Death by Demonstration

Death by Demonstration

Patricia Carlon

First published by Hodder and Stoughton, Limited
in Great Britain in 1970.

Copyright © 1970 by Patricia Carlon.

First published in the United States in 2001 by

Soho Press, Inc.
853 Broadway
New York, NY 10003

Library of Congress Cataloging-in-Publication Data

Carlon, Patricia, 1927–
Death by demonstration / Patricia Carlon.
p. cm.
ISBN 1-56947-246-7 (alk. paper)
1. Vietnamese Conflict, 1961–1975—Protest movements—
Australia—Fiction. 2. Private investigators—Australia—Fiction.
3. Demonstrations—Fiction. 4. Australia—Fiction. I. Title.

PR9619.3.C37 D4 2001
823'.914—dc21   00-050529

10   9   8   7   6   5   4   3   2   1

CHAPTER ONE

The letters that came to him were all shapes and sizes and colours, but all were an appeal for help. Only one thing made the one he held stand out from the others that Tuesday morning—it was unsigned.

The black type demanded curtly, "WHY DID ROBYN CALDER DIE, AND HOW?" It stated, beneath the typed capitals of the question, "She was hit by something the doctors describe as heavy and thin, and probably iron or steel, as no wood particles were found in the wound—something resembling a thin iron bar ... so they *say*. No one had anything like that. They would have been crazy to have had something like that. No one else was hit in that way. No one else died. Robyn Calder did. Why? What killed her? Who struck the blow? The police say the case is closed. Why? They took plenty of action, asked plenty of questions, when it was suggested one of *them* killed her. They say that's impossible. Policemen don't carry iron bars. It wasn't a truncheon—a police truncheon—that killed her. They've made that clear from medical evidence. Clear to all the world, to their own satisfaction. So now the case is closed except for the inquest, unless someone comes forward and says, '*I* struck the blow. *I* struck the blow that killed young Robyn', and there's somewhere they can lay the blame.

"They're doing just that, now. All the world points a finger and says, '*You* killed young Robyn. All of you who were involved'. Do you think that's fair? None of them carried an iron bar. That's ridiculous. It was a peaceful demonstration. No one was armed—except the police. So—how did Robyn die? Who struck the blow?"

Jefferson Shields shook his grey head. One thin hand removed the spectacles from his long nose. He leaned back in the grey chair and his grey eyes surveyed the grey-washed walls of the small room. All the greyness, the insipid water-colour that broke the monotony of one grey wall, were part of an illusion that had been carefully planned not to distract the eye or the thoughts of anyone sitting in the grey high-backed chair opposite the desk. Seated there, with only the greyness and the colourless personality he had deliberately created for himself, they betrayed themselves—their thoughts turned inwards, and their expressions revealed far more than the words spoken across the desk.

This time, though, there was no one to question, or speak out, no one to consider with thoughtful eyes—just a sheet of white paper, with black typing, and a cutting pinned to one corner of it—the whole of it unsigned.

He wondered if the writer had ever considered that they had wasted time and effort; had ever thought that no one had any use for a client who was merely a ghost, an unsigned letter, a black-typed question. Ghosts didn't pay the rent or the telephone bill, or the cost of his office or secretary...

A wry little smile touched his mouth. He slipped the spectacles into place on his thin nose. He could see the cutting clearly then without lifting it from the desk. He continued to lean back in the grey comfortable chair, reading it, though it told him nothing more than he remembered himself from news items in the press.

Condensed, there had been a march of students through the city. They had carried hand-lettered, home-made placards of the usual type. These particular placards had demanded the release of a conscientious objector named Oliver Harrap.

No one had paid more than the briefest attention to them, according to the press. Jefferson Shields amended that, from his own experience. He could clearly picture the frowns, the irritated comments, the half-taunts, and the occasional jostling of the marchers, but none of that, the ordinary resentment of ordinary people, would have been noticed by the marchers, Shields was sure. Armoured in

6

the righteousness of their cause, they had marched through the city to one of the government offices, and there spread themselves out over footpaths and roadways, on stairways and in the building's foyer, holding the placards high, as shields of defiance and righteousness, for all to view.

Perhaps there had been laughter, ironic comments, fairly good-natured banter thrown at them; perhaps even a few congratulatory words, and then, when they had doggedly sat on, disrupting traffic and ordinary life, the laughter would have gone, and the banter and the jests, too. A bald press cutting told so little, he thought ruefully. It couldn't spare words to describe the slow gathering of crowds, and the growing resentment, the first demand of, "Why don't the police shift them?" and then the voices growing louder and louder, and then the first blow, the first thing thrown, the first yells and the first anxious press forward of police.

All that had happened that summer morning when Robyn Calder had died. The demonstration had erupted, like so many others, into real violence. When the building and streets were cleared again of students, everyone had time to see the flotsam left behind—the torn placards, torn clothing, a litter of discarded pamphlets of one sort and another—and a dead girl; and who had killed young Robyn?

The only fact known was that she had been struck violently over the head, and the blow had killed her. The students had howled of police brutality, a howl that had died to bitter mutters when medical evidence made it plain no police truncheon had struck the blow. Shields, staring at the cutting, knew it was unlikely that the mutters would ever completely die, so long as Robyn Calder was remembered anywhere. He wondered if by now the girl had taken on the gloss, in some quarters, of a martyr. He sat still, wondering many other things.

Finally he pressed the bell at his side. He still went on gazing at the cutting, even when the door had opened and closed behind the girl and she had come to stand the other side of the desk, waiting for him to acknowledge she was there.

7

He was uncomfortable with Ann Aveyard. Sometimes he suspected she knew it quite well. It remained a puzzle to him, the fact that Mrs. Gold, his usual secretary, had presented him with Ann on her departure on holidays. He had left it to her common sense to find him a substitute. His first sight of Ann, with her long swinging blonde hair, and the brief skim of dark skirt round her thighs, had been a shock. Not that there was anything wrong with her work. He could admit that without grudging. Her first week had been a success. The office had run almost as smoothly as when Mrs. Gold had presided, till now.

That was the point that rankled, as he continued gazing down at the cutting and letter on the desk. He was annoyed, and a little alarmed. He wondered if the brief skim of skirt would flounce out of the room and out through the office beyond and through the main door, once he spoke.

Finally he lifted his gaze. Her face was expressionless, the perfect picture of an attentive private secretary. The square-framed, dark-rimmed spectacles added to the air of efficient perfection. Not even the brief skirt and the long fall of blonde, swinging hair detracted from the picture.

He asked, "Why didn't you sign your name?"

Two lines creased in the smooth white forehead. When she didn't answer, his hand touched the letter and cutting. He asked again, "Why didn't you sign your name to this? What was the point of sending me an unsigned letter? I don't solve puzzles for fun. I solve them for bread and butter. Why did you imagine this would impress me?" His finger flicked the cutting again. "Did you really expect I would thrust aside all my other letters and concentrate on this one? When it offered me no profit, no client, and no signature?" Impatiently he added, "You typed it on the machine in this office, and on my paper. Also," one grey eyebrow rose in pained enquiry, "in my time?"

Abruptly she laughed. He hadn't expected that. He had shrunk from her possible walking out on him, or her anger, or even tears. With her blonde head thrown back and her round face laughing, she looked much younger, much less efficient and much more human.

8

She said, "Mrs. Gold warned me you noticed everything. I've made a proper hash of it, haven't I?" The fact didn't seem to disconcert her at all. "I suppose I was a bit of a nut to do it that way, but ... I couldn't bring myself to face you, you see, and say outright, 'Look, I've a frightful problem and I quite desperately want you to give me an answer to it, because it's terribly important—to a whole lot of people, but to be completely frank no one involved has any money and I haven't, either, so will you do it for nothing?'" She leaned forward, the laughter gone in tight, hard anxiety that made even her voice more strident when she asked, "Is bread and butter so terribly important to you that you could never, never solve something for someone who can't pay you?"

The knowledge that she had neatly forced him into a corner angered him. He said coldly, "You knew very well I would recognise the type and the paper and know who had sent that letter. What possible purpose ..."

"Lots. If I'd come to you and started my question, and admitted there was no money in it for you, you wouldn't have listened, in all probability. Would you have?" She brushed that aside without waiting for an answer. "But now you've read the question and you're remembering about Robyn Calder and you know what it's all about, so I've got facts through to you that I mightn't even have managed to say otherwise, because you might not only have closed your ears, quite finally, but you might have handed me my wages and told me the door was over thataway and would I please go through and not come back. This way, you might still do it, but you've read those facts and you won't stop thinking about it—even if I go, because you're angered, and the anger will stay and needle at you and ..."

He laughed. He hadn't meant to, and beneath the laughter was a decided respect. Shrewdness, he reflected approvingly, and smartness and a decided degree of courage. That added up to a certain measure of desperation. So Robyn Calder's death meant a whole measure of things to her.

He put the question aloud, demanding, "Why is it so

9

important the police continue enquiring into the Calder case?"

The taut lines of her body relaxed. A quite audible sigh of relief escaped her lips and unconsciously she leaned back in the grey chair. He thought dispassionately that she was telling herself that she had him hooked, even if that hook might later pull free, so that she would have to try other measures to keep his interest, and help.

She said slowly, "I know a lot of the students involved."

"A lot? Or one in particular?"

Her shoulders lifted again. "That, too."

"And?" He waited patiently while she hesitated.

At last she said, "Robyn Calder died six weeks ago. It doesn't seem that long because of all that's been happening. First there were the police enquiries. That took up a lot of everyone's time, and there's been dodging reporters and silly fools who seem to think that if they express sympathy they'll get Nigel and the others to start another row about police methods and all that sort of thing. Then there's been a University enquiry. That was worst of all really, and it hasn't finished yet and no one yet knows what's going to happen. And there's the inquest. The University is waiting for that. So's the public. And the police. The press, too. It's all going to be rehashed again and what's going to be everyone's verdict?

"No one can settle to work and lectures. They're all wondering what's going to happen. There's been ... well, pressure, that's the best word I can think of to describe it ... but someone's head is going to roll. That's what Nigel says. Someone has to be made a scapegoat. There was too much bad publicity, you see, and the only way to stop the pressure, the anger, the bitterness, is for the University to punish someone—to point a finger and say, 'Well, we don't know who struck the blow, but we know who started that demonstration and that's you, so out you go.' Are you following me?" she demanded anxiously.

"Oh yes. Some action has to be taken to appease public outrage, even if the action, to those close to events, is hardly going to appear justice. It's the public who must feel that justice is being done."

"That's it exactly, and you see..."

"Who is this Nigel you mention?" he broke in.

The question seemed to fluster her. Then she said, "Nigel Detrick."

The name meant nothing to him, but he asked, "He is studying ... what?"

"Arts. He wants to go on to Law," the answer was given impatiently. "You see..."

"Is he a particular friend of this..." he glanced down at the cutting, "this Oliver Harrap?"

"Yes. They were at school together. They planned on doing University together, but Oliver failed his first exams. He'd been paying too much attention to outside things, I think, because actually he's quite brilliant. He was in the national service ballot and his name was drawn and when he failed the exams they wouldn't give him another deferment of course. He was called up and he wouldn't go, so they jailed him. You must have read about it?"

"Yes. Was Nigel Detrick, then, the ringleader in this demonstration?"

"I suppose so." Hastily she added, "I know that sounds crazy, but actually it had no real leader, according to Nigel. There were discussions and talks and a plan was evolved and others were drawn in, and it was really a round circle of people who were interested in the problem and sorry for Oliver, who took action together, but of course everyone knows Nigel and Oliver were the closest of friends, so it's natural they've all jumped to the conclusion that Nigel planned the whole thing."

"That being so, Detrick is in the position where his head may well be the one to roll in sacrifice?"

"Yes." Her hands were twisting at each other. "It's ridiculous, outrageous rather, that just because the public wants a scapegoat to salve everyone's conscience about Robyn Calder, that someone like Nigel should be tossed on the scrapheap. He's clever, and he's done marvellously well in exams, but that's going to count for nothing, unless ... look," her hands were spread out to him now in appeal, "none of them—not a single one—had any sort of weapon that morning. Nigel's sworn to me by everything under the sun that that's the truth. He says that because there's been violence in the past they were terribly careful to make sure that this demonstration would be peaceful. They actually *searched* everyone of the students who were going to march. Not one of them had any sort of weapon. They didn't," her voice shook with a laughter that was close to tears, "even have so much as a rotten tomato on them. Nigel's told me all that, and told it to others, over and over again, and the other students back him up, but no one outside of myself is willing to believe it."

"You prefer the theory of police brutality?" he suggested dryly, "and the idea that the doctors are covering up for them? I notice you've underlined the word 'say' when referring offered medical evidence for my inspection. Don't you accept that medical evidence?"

She hesitated, began, "Oh, I ..." then she shook her head and admitted, "yes, I accept it. I've tried not to, because blaming the police is easiest, you see, but ... I don't believe in that idea at all. Nigel doesn't, either."

"What do you imagine happened then?" When she didn't answer he suggested, "You think that someone from outside the University—a trouble-maker, came armed, to break up the demonstration, to cause the riot that happened, and that Robyn Calder got in his way?" When there was still no answer he objected, "It would be impossible to prove such an idea. Such a person would have come from obscurity, to return to obscurity till there was another chance of causing trouble. There is, of course, the type of person who revels in violence—who might see such a demonstration as a chance of letting off his violent feelings. Such people do exist, and probably they do cause part of the trouble in these types of disturbance, but ... where do you find such a person? Unless he was seen—unless his weapon was seen ..."

He knew the sudden eagerness in her expression was going to be reflected in her voice and words when she spoke and he dampened it with a chilling, "And if any person had seen such a weapon, such a person, they would surely have come forward. Remember there has been great public indignation over this girl's unfortunate death. Anyone who has anything to give in the way of information about that morning has come forward—the press reports have spoken of that."

The eagerness had drained away. She sat quite still, the blonde head bent, looking down at her hands. After a little he asked, quite gently, "What do you want me to do?"

She looked up then. Her gaze seemed abstracted, far-away. She said slowly, "I don't think I honestly know—oh, except I had some idea you might perform a miracle. It was stupid, of course, but I've been so scared and Nigel ... he's altered, you see. He's thinner, but that's a small point really. It's ... it's *inside* him, is the big change. He seems to have given up already, and he's hard and bitter and ... it's not helping of course," she shook her head vehemently. "It's only making things worse when they question him, because he seems sullen and angry and bitter, where he should be humble and afraid perhaps—oh..." she thrust her hands apart impatiently, "I can't explain, but he's changed and I hate it and all this ... this *witch-hunting*, this yearning for a victim because she's dead ... it's horrible.

"If only they'd be willing to believe about the search— that none of them was armed ... that'd be something, but no one wants to believe anything at all that the students say. They're just closing their minds to it, as the police have apparently closed their enquiries. The police say they're leaving it now to the University, and the University is leaving it to the public to judge and ... the public's going to demand blood, after the inquest. If the police would only keep the enquiry open—make it seem they were doing something to find some outsider..."

He knew it was really a question, a pleading, for him to face the police. Her expression said that while they wouldn't listen to herself, or to Nigel Detrick, they might listen to Jefferson Shields.

He sighed. He didn't want involvement. There was a

bad taste in his mouth already from discussing it, he reflected wryly and the whole thing seemed pointless. He had given her blunt facts—a faceless outsider would be impossible to find, and the public indignation wasn't going to be appeased by the faceless, the unknown.

She urged, "Would you speak to Nigel?"

"Why?" he asked bluntly.

"Mrs. Gold told me you pride yourself on knowing if a person is speaking truth or lies to your face. You'll know, if you question Nigel, if he's lying or not. About that search for one thing. About the other points, too. If you're sure he's telling the truth, couldn't you go to the police then and urge them to keep the case open, to . . ."

He knew amusement, and respect again, for the ground work she'd done—all the questions about him that she had asked of Mrs. Gold, all the planning and scheming.

He said, simply out of that respect for her planning and courage, "Very well, I'll talk to them."

CHAPTER TWO

Jefferson Shields knew quite well that she had had a long debate with herself as to the wisdom of bringing him to the place. She had, he was quite certain, pictured him standing out like a freak among the students, among the jeans and shirts and the shrill youthful voices, so that the voices would become quiet, and eyes would slant sideways at them, till they became the focus of everyone's attention.

He knew, too, that she was surprised now, that it hadn't happened—that in his neat grey suit, and neat grey shoes, with his grey head and colourless, ordinary features, he had sunk into nothingness, become nothing more than a shadow against the brightly painted wall behind his chair.

She was nervous, as well as surprised. Her gaze kept going to the stairs curving away upwards out of sight to the street level above them. She kept saying, and every time the words held a further stress, a further anxiety, as though she was hoping they were going to prove true and that she wasn't going to be let down, "He'll come soon. He promised."

He made no answer to the breathless assurances. He simply sat, hands linked on the glass top of the tiny table, looking about them. There was noise, plenty of it, but it was an orderly noise, once the sounds were sorted one from another. There was the overriding clatter of china and cutlery, the hiss of the coffee urn, the slap-slap of the waitresses' flat-soled shoes on the tiled floor, the shrillness of voices, and a background of slow-tempo music. People came and went up and down the stairs—a steady flow up and down of colour that was one minute vibrant and one minute dead browns and blacks. The one overriding impression was youth. Even the waitresses, the boy at the cash desk, looked too young to be in the business world at all.

One of the girls slap-slapped her way to their table, slid filled coffee cups in front of them and the check—a red ticket with two scrawled figures on the face—in front of Shields. Sliding it under the saucer, out of the way, he sipped the coffee.

He broke his silence for the first time, breaking across Ann Aveyard's breathless, "He promised..." with, "Who owns this place?"

"Owns...? I don't know. Why?"

"Simple curiosity. My mind turning on facts dealing with bread and butter, you might say. The coffee is excellent, the price—so I should have thought—too low for a profitable venture."

Her shoulders lifted impatiently. She said curtly, "If it wasn't good and wasn't cheap, the students wouldn't come. When you've only a bit of money you have to make certain you're going to get value for every cent of it. That's plain common sense. There's always a crowd like this. You multiply that by the profit on every customer and I reckon you'd come out the right side of the ledger." She went on talking. He was aware that it was talk for the sake of breaking the silence, to steady herself against the anxiety of waiting. Then abruptly her cup clattered back into the saucer and she stood up, so sharply the little table rocked and nearly upset, but she never noticed it, or Shields' exclamation, and his quick move to hold the table still.

Her gaze was fixed on the stairway, and she was smiling waving to the man who stood on the third stair from the top, looking down.

He didn't wave back, but simply centred his gaze on the waving girl, then went on down the stairs and across to them. He stood for a minute towering over the tiny table, then reached for an adjoining vacant chair, slid it across and sat down. The space was so narrow that his broad shoulders nearly touched the two who already sat there, on either side.

He gazed steadily at the older man and said, "I'm Nigel Detrick."

"Nigel..." the girl began, but he gave a little shake of his dark head at her, without looking at her, his gaze still holding the other man's, and she fell silent, waiting.

"Well?" His voice was deep and pleasant and faintly mocking, "How do I sum up, Mr. Shields?"

Jefferson Shields didn't answer. He went on with his slow, calculating scrutiny of each feature, from the long face with the darkish scuff of beard, to the big nose jutting above the wide mouth, and the dark brown—almost black —eyes under thick dark brows. He noted the sun-darkened skin and, surprising fact in a student, the broken-nailed hands, scarred and scratched in one or two places.

The boy's gaze followed his, centred on the big hands. He spread them out flat for inspection. Abruptly he grinned. "Surprised I do some manual work? Pampered, a lot of people call us. They say that if we had to earn our living with hard labour it'd do us good, instead of us getting everything for free. You believe that? It's not true, you know. You wouldn't get much of a pampered life on university allowances. I work weekends. Hard work. Clearing land for people wanting to build houses. You get your nails broken and your hands scratched and blistered. You get backache, and bitten by spiders and sometimes you get ticks on you, and once I've even disturbed a black snake and narrowly saved my legs from trouble. You call that pampering?"

"No. Educational. You know now how to kill a snake, and how to clear land for your own home when you want to build for yourself."

Abruptly the boy laughed. The hard defiance vanished. He looked younger and a lot more pleasant with his mouth overcoming its hard lines.

Jefferson Shields demanded, "How do you find time, between land clearing and lectures and studying, to attend these demonstrations?"

The boy crossed his arms on the table top. He said curtly, "If you're interested enough in something there's always time to be scraped up somewhere."

"So the question of Oliver Harrap's imprisonment was of

17

deep interest and concern to you?"

"Yes. Mind you, I'm not saying that Harry—I always call him that—that Harry didn't make a mess of things, but jailing him—good God, where's the point of it?" he demanded impatiently. "Jailing's supposed to reform a man from a life of crime. What crime's Harry committed? I suppose in there he'll be eating and working with men who've been put in there for killing someone. So—he gets shot in because he doesn't want to kill anyone. You show me the sense in that. Isn't there something cock-eyed about it to your reasoning?"

"He wasn't jailed for refusing to kill anyone. He was jailed for refusing to obey the law," Shields pointed out mildly. "Possibly in there he will be forced to associate with men who have stolen from those who've befriended them in the past. The country has befriended Oliver Harrap in the past, and cherished him and cared for him, and then he intended to defraud it of the two years service he owed it." He said blandly, gently, to the surprised face opposite, "It's surprising how one can make a valid argument for anything at all, from all sides of any matter. I don't claim that I am right, or that you are, or that Oliver Harrap is. I am merely pointing out that you can make a valid argument from all sides of a question, if you think hard enough."

For a minute there was silence, then slowly the young man relaxed, leaning back in the chair. He said at last, "That was clever, and well reasoned. I shan't try and tangle arguments with you, and they don't matter anyway, do they? The rights and the wrongs don't matter at all. Just accept that that morning six weeks ago I thought I was right, that I thought it was wrong Harry was in jail, that I thought it a waste and a stupidity and a cruelty and a whole lot of other things that boiled down to injustice. A lot of us thought the same way. We wanted to show people how we felt. We wanted them to know a wrong had been done. We wanted to get their support.

"You know," the broken-nailed hand traced a little circle round and round on the glass table-top, "when you've a lot of money you can make a fuss and people are inclined to listen—because you've money; because you represent a certain status of living, a certain power because of what you can buy. The same with being an adult. You've reached a certain status in society. But a student—it's different then. You've no status at all; no power of money or maturity. All you have is a loud voice, and yourself. Oh well," he brushed that aside, "leave that. It's not important. We keep getting side-tracked. The point is, we wanted people—the people who have status and a bit of power—to take notice—to sit up and listen to us and do something to help Harry. So we had that demonstration. It was to be a perfectly peaceful, orderly thing. Wait," he added sharply, "before you comment, or start picking holes in that, give me a hearing. We had it all planned. We made placards and we carried them. Nothing else. Not a single thing at all. Not one of us had the simplest weapon. We walked in double file on the outside of the footway from the gathering point to where we intended to halt. There were to be speeches to anyone who'd stop and listen to us. There was going to be no real obstruction. Oh yes, we sat on the footpaths and the roads and the stairs, just as the press said we did. We weren't obstructive, to my mind. We left a clear passage down the centre of the footpath and up the stairway and inside the building, and on the road we occupied the space that would have been taken by three parked cars, and if you want to know, we put ten cents in the meters. Didn't that entitle us to park ourselves instead of our cars?

"I put that argument to the police afterwards, but it didn't get anywhere. Evidently cars are more important than people. I asked them then, how much it took to park a body by a parking meter so that I'd know next time. Wasn't that perfectly reasonable? I got told to belt up and to stop giving cheek.

"Where's the justice in that? I fail to see it. If we'd come along, packed in cars, and parked them there at those meters, we'd have been law-abiding, but because we omitted the cars, we weren't."

The passion and bitterness went from his voice and face.

Abruptly he laughed. He suggested, "You find me a valid argument for the other side of the case, hmm?"

"It is an offence for people to linger on roadways, or walk on them where an adequate footway is provided. The road is for vehicular traffic. It is an offence for vehicular traffic to trespass on a footway; and an offence for a pedestrian to linger on a roadway." The answer was given in faint mockery, faint amusement, that brought a laughing rejoinder from the other.

Sobering, he said, "Some day I'd honestly like to have the chance to debate with you—open forum—at the University club." The laughter was completely gone when he added, "Though at the moment it looks very much like I mightn't be around much longer to debate with anyone. We've sidetracked again, haven't we? Back to that morning then—we thought we were doing right, added to which we thought we'd taken all precautions for a peaceful demonstration." He lifted his gaze. The eyes seemed darker than ever as he said quietly, "None of us had any weapons at all. There was a search. We had nothing."

"What about the placards? Were they attached to poles, sticks, to..."

"Most definitely not. Hand-held. If you have them on poles you're asking for trouble. Some hot-head will make a grab for one, and a struggle starts. Usually hot-head gets the placard, plus pole and he'll use it to crack anybody down who tries getting the placard back. You've only to look at newsreels, TV shots and press photos to see just what trouble a pole can be. I tell you it was meant to be peaceful. We *planned* for it to go off smoothly and without one scrap of trouble. We..."

"Then what went wrong?"

The big shoulders slumped. For the first time his gaze slid away. He said helplessly, "I don't know. It's useless saying that someone threw a punch and the one punched threw one back and so on and so on and on and *on*. We were ready for that sort of thing. No one was going to throw a punch back. No matter how provoked. We were going to take it. Harry had gone to jail on the grounds of

20

being a Conshie. He'd refused war service—the hitting back at an enemy. If we were going to have a demonstration backing him up we'd lose the whole force of it if the first time we got a blow we promptly jumped up and started bashing back.

"It was going to be a case of us all turning the other cheek. All of us knew the score and we'd all agreed to take the risk of a punching-up, a good belting, anything any hot-head wanted to hand out to us. A few of the crowd backed out for that very reason. They didn't think they could take it. That was fine. We didn't want any waverers with us."

"So Robyn Calder wasn't a waverer? She was heartily backing you? She was an opponent of violence?"

He hesitated, looking down at his hands, frowning slightly. He said at last, "Robyn was a funny kid. Oh, I don't mean humorous. Odd is what I meant. She had wild enthusiasms that never lasted long. For a week, for two weeks, even longer, she'd be so engrossed in one special thing you couldn't get sense out of her on any other subject, and then, one morning you'd mention that special subject and she'd look at you as though she hadn't a clue what you were babbling about, then she'd say something along the lines of, 'Oh that—I just didn't see my way to going along with that any more.' You never got reasons, just the blunt fact that whatever it was had ceased to goad her.

"That day—well, she was in the middle of a wild drive against violence, capital punishment—the whole bang lot. There were no half measures about young Robyn. When she fixed her teeth into something she took the whole thing in one gulp. Sometimes you never could tell what set off the spark in one direction, but I do think I know what had her mind fixed on non-violence that particular time.

"She'd been in another demonstration a while before. That was against police handling of yet another demonstration against conscription—some of the kids got hauled off pretty roughly. This one she was in turned really nasty and she had a fright when one fool started to bash in another's face. They weren't students or part of the demonstration at all. They were just a couple of hot-heads getting a bit of violence out of their gut. Robyn was scared solid and who'd blame her—after all the sight of a pulped face isn't pleasant. She ran away. She tried getting shelter in shops and buildings, but they weren't having any part of her. Who'd blame them? It was a student demonstration and she was obviously a student. How'd they know she wasn't out for trouble, getting someone to let her in so that a whole mob would stream in and beat the place up? That's the way people think about us, you must admit.

"Robyn was badly shocked by it all. For the next few days she crept around wailing to anyone who'd listen, about the evils of violence. Our demonstration was tailored to measure for her feelings right then. She jumped in with both feet. Like I told you, when a craze was on her she was wildly enthusiastic. We needed as many marchers as we could rally, and she seemed the most anti-violence person in the place."

His voice fell to bitterness, "Which makes it worse that she was the one to get into trouble. I keep picturing it, you know—a useless exercise and unprofitable and stupid, too—but I can't get away from it. Have you ever been in a kangaroo shoot?" At the other's shake of head, he went on slowly, "I have. Just once. Once was plenty. It was out west. I don't think the brutes had ever seen much of men before. Not men with guns anyway. They just stood there, staring at us with big dark innocent eyes, and they had their brains blasted out for their trust. I keep thinking of that and of Robyn—right then she was against violence. She might have stood just that way—just staring with big innocent eyes, waiting—and she got her head bashed in for it.

"Oh yes," impatiently his voice rose, though Shields hadn't tried to speak, "it was an accident. I know it. No one meant to kill her or hurt her either. She just got in the road, but still..."

"Who found her? First noticed she didn't get up? First tried to help her, went to her?"

"The police I think. They'd brought the paddy waggon up by then and were bundling us in. I was inside myself.

I certainly saw them bend to someone on the ground, and they didn't move, and then they straightened up and one called something and ... I think he was a sergeant—I can never remember how many stripes to what—but he was obviously a senior man—and he went over. My view got shut off then. They closed the waggon doors on us and drove us away. We never learned till much later that she was dead."

"Where was she lying? Had she been in the centre of the trouble? On the outskirts? You said that in a previous demonstration she had run away. Do you think it possible she might have attempted to run from the scene this time, also and had been stopped—thrust back by someone..."

"Can't I make you believe, understand, rely on the fact that none of us were armed?" He sounded tired now, and his gaze was once more back on his big, scarred hands. "You're trying to make out that one of us might have resented a deserter and given her a good clout to herd her back. Forget it. It wasn't that way. We weren't armed—with anything bar our hands, and she wasn't hit that way. That point for a starter, and then another—no one was conscripted into that march." His gaze rose and mocked at Shields' former argument, "It wasn't the law that she owed the rest of us to stay and see it out. She wouldn't have been jailed for deserting. She could have left any point, any street, any moment she liked."

He was silent for a little while, then said quietly, "But have you thought of this? We were rounded up and shoved in the paddy waggon. Higgledy-piggledy—it was a case of the law's hand reaching for the nearest body that looked like it belonged to a student, and they didn't let go. Maybe, if it seemed like she was going to get out of the circle they'd made round us, they'd give her a shove back. Wouldn't they?"

"With what? It wasn't a police truncheon that killed her," he was reminded sharply.

"They might have grabbed at something—anything to hand—to use to protect themselves. They might ..."

"So might any of the students." Shields' voice held a weary impatience. "No, don't parade your arguments again.

23

I accept that, so far as you know, the students had no intention of violence, but it's extremely hard, however firm your intentions, to face actual violence without some form of resistance or protection. A moment's panic, an outstretched hand, something to grip at, and a man can be armed before he is aware of what he is doing. You faced violence yourself. What was your reaction? Can you honestly claim that at no point whatsoever did you use your fists, your elbows, your feet ..."

"I claim it." The voice was tight and hard. "I claim it and I mean it. I wasn't the speaker that day. I sat down on the steps. I've told you—the whole thing was planned down to the last detail. When violence started I kept my place. How else do you think I was put in the paddy waggon? How else do you think the police arrested as many of us as they did? It was because we made no resistance at all. I simply sat. So did others around me. I can't speak for everyone because there were people tumbling over us and fighting on top of us, but I didn't move. The police simply picked me up and tossed me into the waggon."

This is madness, Shields told himself, gazing down into the empty coffee cup, to avoid the searching dark gaze trying to hold his. I'm getting nowhere, because there's nowhere to go. He asked, "When did you last see the girl? Was she sitting near you? Did she march beside you?"

"No, to both questions." The answer came promptly. "I've thought about that point a lot. Where did I see her last? Who was with her then? Did I catch a glimpse of anyone who *might* have been Robyn? Have what I've dredged up." He thrust the big scarred hands across the table, palms upwards, as though the answer was there, given freely, to the other man. "I saw her when we lined up at the starting point. She was about half way along the line. I was near the top. Four times I can remember looking back while we marched and seeing her. No, there was nothing distinctive about her dress that day. She was wearing fawn coloured slacks, sneakers and a green jacket over a shirt—much the same as the other girls. It just happened, though, that she was the only girl in that group—there were men all round

24

her and I picked out that long hair and short figure among the men.

"I saw her again when we settled down. She was near one of the parking meters, but once she was sitting I lost her in the crowd. Anyway I wasn't paying attention to that area. I was waiting for the speeches to start.

"I can't dredge up another single sight of her. Even that figure on the ground—it was just a figure—just a pair of sneakers really and socks. It could have been a man, a girl—I couldn't tell.

"I know what you'll ask next—who saw her last? We've talked that over, endlessly. It seems to be Graham Whitty. The police came and ordered the crowd off the road, then started throwing them off. There was no arresting just then —they just picked the kids up and dumped them on the pavement. They tossed Robyn on to Whitty, and he had the wind knocked out of him. When he'd shoved her off his stomach and had his wind back, she was on her feet, shifting back towards the fountain and the building. Look, have you ever been there? Do you know what the scene was like?" His big hand began to sketch on the table. "There's the road, then the pavement, then a stretch of space in front of the building, and close to the building there's a fountain, with some rockery around it, and then you go sideways towards the building and the stairway.

"Whitty says he thought she was going to sit with us on the steps and he tried to follow, but couldn't. There were police and pedestrians and students all mixed up together and all in a bad temper, so he just flopped down again on the pavement and stayed put till they carried him away."

"Where was she found?"

"Huddled against the building, near the fountain."

"How long did all this take? How long after you settled down did the police start moving the students from the road-way? How long after that till the end of it?"

"Could *you* gauge time correctly in a mess like that?" Detrick demanded. "I couldn't, anyway. You could try working it out for yourself. We arrived. We settled. That took a few minutes, because we were careful to leave those spaces on the footwalk and up the stairs for people to pass us. I can't say how many minutes, but several.

"Next, the first speaker took his place close to me and started speaking. He must have spoken about a hundred words when the police moved in to ask the crowd on the road to shift. He stopped speaking then, as everyone's attention was the road. There was a bit of chit-chat between police and students—another few minutes there I expect, then the police started hefting them up and shoving them on to the pavement and some of the bystanders started laughing, because as fast as one student was dumped, he got up and went back to the road, to sit down again.

"That was when the trouble started. Like I said, there were pedestrians and bystanders and police and students all in a muddle. I suppose someone threw a punch to get through and next thing a brawl was going on and a few women started screaming. There was one in the building right behind us yipping away as though she'd been raped, yet there wasn't a thing going on anywhere close to her.

"The police heard her, though. Some of them turned, and it was natural enough for them to imagine there was real trouble going on inside the building where they couldn't see, so they started fighting their way through to it.

"After that..." he shrugged helplessly, "it was just a mess. Time? It was impossible to time anything. Impossible for any of us to try and stop the brawling either. Impossible to do anything but sit it out."

"Don't you think it equally impossible to ask me to pinpoint a figure in that mêlée of people—police, pedestrians, bystanders, students—and say quite definitely that that particular person was the cause of Robyn Calder dying? You must admit yourself that if none of you who were present and saw it happening can help pinpoint anyone, that it would be ridiculous to ask me to do it. Why did you ... or rather, Miss Aveyard ... bring me into it?" His thoughts were already moving away from them both, and from his surroundings, back to the grey-walled office, to the piled-up correspondence on the desk, and the problems that were, as he had told the girl, bread and butter to him.

His attention was jerked back by the abrupt, "Have you thought that it needn't have been accident at all? That it could have been murder—deliberate murder?"

Shields' grey head jerked up, and the steady challenging dark gaze held his, as the boy asked again, "Have you thought it could be murder? Just give me a hearing— just for five minutes. I know you'll say that now I'm grasping at straws—that I'm trying to get the pressure off myself. Of course I'm trying that, but there's more to the suggestion than that. Have you ever considered—closely—what a *safe* killing it would be. Death by Demonstration, the papers would call it, and you wouldn't so much as have to dispose of the body. All you'd have to do would be go there, and make sure a brawl started, and then get close to your victim and who's going to notice? Who's even going to notice a girl falling and getting trampled? No one did that morning. Then when it's all over you can be a long way away, or just walking away, or ... well, anywhere ... and you're quite safe because it'll all be blamed on to student violence." The dark gaze challenged the older man again, along with the curt, "Well?"

Shields took time to consider it critically. He said at last, "I agree that you've made a point. There would be quite considerable risk, however, unless you were part of that demonstration—unless," now his own gaze held challenge, "unless perhaps you, the murderer, were a student yourself?"

"Yes." The boy was impatient now that he had made the other man listen. He pressed, "I've already gone that far, but isn't there risk attached to any murder? And no matter who you were, if you dressed in jeans and a windcheater and sneakers, put on dark glasses perhaps, ruffled your hair, made a placard to fit in with the demonstration, and waded into it, would anyone notice you? Or recognise you? They wouldn't, you know.

"Now look," his voice coaxed now to hold the other's attention, "there was something queer about young Robyn that last week. No, I'm not making it up. I'm not trying

27

to get that pressure that I've acknowledged, off my shoulders by lying. I'm telling you facts. It wasn't readily noticeable, back then, because she was so queer about her various crazes. We took her oddness for granted, but that last week ... well, the most noticeable fact then of course was her sudden desire to convert the world and bring peace on earth, and condemn all violence and all the rest of it. That was *normal* queerness, you might say, and because it was so noticeable, and so usual for her to be having a craze over something nobody bothered about the rest.

"How this first dawned on me, was us thrashing things over and over, with the police, with the press, at the University, amongst ourselves. It was talk and talk. It has been for these past six weeks, and bit by bit little things came to light and I suddenly realised how odd she had been that last week of her life. Perhaps a lot of things have been exaggerated, perhaps some of the talk was being wise after the event, and perhaps a fair slice has been an attempt to shift pressure off student activities..." He stopped. "I'm speaking badly now, but I'm trying to make you understand that what I'm going to say can't possibly all be just moonshine. There were too many people that the bits and pieces came from, and they gave it independently. There was no putting our heads together and saying, 'Look here, there's a way out if we can make it seem she was murder material.' That hasn't been the way of it at all.

"Normally, Robyn was rather placid and introverted, apart from those crazes of hers. To me they always seemed pathetic—like the crushes girls get on various men— the blokes are everything in the world to them for a space of time and instantly forgotten when a new chap swims into view. I've thought those crazes of hers might have been a substitute for those crushes—but that's head-shrinker talk, isn't it, and a subject I know nothing about, so let's leave it.

"Facts—and that's what you're after—are that Robyn wasn't taken up by the men. Oh, certainly she was drawn into the demonstrations and debates and so on, but always as part of a group. She didn't click with any man in particular. Frankly, there are so many girl students and the men know so many girls outside as well, that unless a girl is very attractive, very interesting, very wealthy or very willing to sleep around, she doesn't do much in the dating line with the University men. Most of the girls have boyfriends outside, but I doubt if Robyn did.

"From things she let fall, her father didn't encourage them. He's a widower and she housekeeps for him. Maybe he didn't want a change of housekeeper, or maybe he was just too protective, but if she went to anything it was always with Calder, though it seemed more often she stayed home of an evening and played chess with him. It sounds cruel. I can't help that, but it was a joke with some of the kids. If a man had got tired of a girl he put it to her she could go and play chess with her dad of an evening from there on." He shrugged that aside and admitted, "You're thinking now that that hardly makes her sound murder material, and I agree, but when her last week of life was something entirely different, doesn't it make you wonder?

"For one thing—she was suddenly trying to find someone to join her in taking a flat. She'd never tried doing that before. Why did she suddenly decide she didn't want to stay home and play chess with dad any more?"

Jefferson Shields' voice was cold. His mind was turning back again towards the comfort of the grey-walled office, and the letters that waited him there. He pointed out, "You've told me over and over again she developed sudden crazes for things. Here was another. A craze to leave home and share a flat. At one time or another I should imagine every eighteen-year-old girl in the country shares an identical wish."

The young face opposite looked quite blank. He admitted, "I expect you're right, but consider it in relation to this other point—all of a sudden there was a man in her life and he meant a whole heap to her, and yet—she didn't want anyone at the University to meet him. She didn't want to talk about him, or tell his name, or mention what he looked like. What do you read into that? It doesn't add up to sense when you think what sort of a girl

Robyn was—a girl who'd never had a boyfriend she could talk about; a girl who stayed home of an evening playing chess with her dad. When that type gets a boyfriend finally she wants to show him off—well," he gave a fleeting grin, "like a trophy—along the lines of, 'Look, I can rope and halter a man too.' You understand?"

At the older man's nod, he went on earnestly, "What was so secret about him and their whole relationship? And what was wrong that knowing him meant she had to leave home? What do you read into that? Because that was the background of her wanting a flat-mate, and *why* a flat-mate? Why not a flat for herself and the man, if everything was on the up and up and they intended to get married? It's all wrong, the way she was acting, isn't it? Another thing, if a girl's close to her family, she wouldn't leave home if she was getting married—she'd be married from home with wedding bells and orange blossom and a three-tier cake. Wouldn't she?

"There was something wrong. None of us would have known there was a man at all, only she went round that way trying to find a flat-mate to set up house with her, and one of the girls got her in a depressed moment for Robyn and asked what it was all about—why she wanted to leave home. Maybe Robyn'd been bottling things up for a long time, because she blurted out that it was because of a man. She said to Chris—Chris Stowe, that is—something like this. 'It's because of a man I've met. I met a complete stranger, out there at a demonstration,' and she waved a hand towards the city's skyline. 'We met, and nothing's ever going to be the same again—for either of us.'

"Chris says she was near to tears, and then she shut up fast. She evidently regretted saying that much. She told Chris that, no, the man wasn't anyone Chris knew, and she added bluntly, defiantly, 'I don't want you to meet him,' and then she marched off. What do you do when someone takes that sort of attitude? You shut up yourself, of course. Chris did, though she was burning up with curiosity, but there was only a few days till Robyn was killed, and she never found out anything.

"But here's something else." He stopped, seemed to be groping for words, and then began again, more slowly, "He never came forward. There was never a mention of him, a sight of him. Don't you think we were all burning with curiosity along with Chris? She'd spoken of that talk with Robyn—said how doubly shocking it made things seem because Robyn was involved with a man, and the girls looked for him at the graveside, at the church service, too. There wasn't a sign of him. No, wait," he urged, "you're going to say we just didn't notice him—that he shrank into the background, but that's not so. There was her father and half a dozen vague cousins—a few of the girls got an introduction to them, so they know who they were—standing around with respectfully grieved faces, and most of them obviously wishing they hadn't need come at all. There was the University crowd who'd known her, and there was the clergyman and a couple of neighbours from her street at home.

"There wasn't anyone else. It was a private affair. There was a dreadful sort of humour about the whole thing. Because of the publicity and the uproar about her death the time and the place and the day was a secret. Some little black-edged cards went to just a few of the girls—ones she'd taken home at times. They were invites to the funeral, set up for all the world like party invitations, with an R.S.V.P. in the corner, and the statement admittance was by invitation card only.

"I suppose I'm being too critical—that that was the only way to work things, but—you must admit there was a dreadful sort of humour about the little cards."

He stopped, obviously waiting for the older man to say something. When there was no comment he looked disappointed. The broad shoulders moved in a quick shrug, then he went on, "So you can understand there weren't many people at all, and they were all accounted for—the University girls, and the neighbours and the vague cousins. There was no sign of a single man—a man who should have been standing beside Dad Calder, as a bereaved prospective bridegroom.

31

"Chris asked. Quite brazenly. She asked, 'Didn't Robyn have a special boyfriend?' and she got the answer that no, there wasn't anyone like that at all.

"How does that fit in with the things she said—the way she was acting that last week?"

Shields said, "You're considering, of course, the possibility of a married man. She would never mention such a man to her father, or be able to take him home, or show him to her friends, or boast about her friendship with him. She could never even meet him to take their friendship further, unless she was living away from home. A flat, with a flat-mate to settle the parents' doubts, is the usual thing in such a case. The flat-mate conveniently absents herself at suitable times and the girl entertains—unsuitably. Quite so. That set-up is as old as sin." He demanded, "But where does that make her murder material?"

"Consider it in relationship to the fact that maybe she was beginning to want a more permanent, more settled, more privileged affair with the chap, just when he was deciding he was tired of the game. She met him at a demonstration, but how long ago was that? It's ten months since she took part in her first one, and parked cars and back seats are as old as sin, too, you know." He gave a lop-sided grin. "But they're apt to pall—and just as old as sin and the flat away from home set-up is the sad tale of a girl who is trying to hold a man when he's trying to say, 'It's been nice knowing you, but the party's over and I'm going home to the wife and kids.'

"Maybe the try for a flat was a try at holding him, a try for something better than a parked car—a try for a few home comforts and dinners for two and whole evenings in comfort, and he wasn't having any. If he turned down the proposition and she turned nasty, and he wanted to keep his marriage without any ructions, what could he do?"

The dark eyes were sparkling, his tanned face flushed with earnestness and excitement. The big broken-nailed fingers were tapping impatiently on the glass table-top, waiting for the older man to speak. When there was only a discouraging silence, he cried angrily, "If she was trying to kid herself the writing wasn't on the wall for their affair that'd account for her up and down moods, wouldn't it? And the flat idea was her last chance to hold him, while leaving home without Dad Calder getting suspicious. Then, if the man was in a corner, and he saw a chance to get rid of her—to fake a death by demonstration—why shouldn't he have taken it?"

Jefferson Shields demanded, "Have you considered that the girl must have been well aware of the derision, the laughing behind her back, of the comments to other girls to stay home of an evening and play chess with their father? Don't ask me to believe that none of that derision ever came to her ears. You have admitted yourself there was latent cruelty in that, but you've apparently over-looked the effect it might have on a sensitive, introverted girl.

"She might well have decided that her father was too protective, too sheltering and her home life too restrictive. Isn't it possible that she told herself that if only she had more freedom she would have boyfriends for the choosing? It would be a hard and difficult decision for a girl of her type to walk out on a widowed father. Her up and down moods would be clearly accounted for by her wavering from going ahead or staying put."

"To Chris Stowe . . ."

"Oh yes, she confided—apparently—to Chris Stowe. I say apparently and I mean that. She was in a depressed state. She was near tears. They are your own words. What caused that? Had she been rebuffed by some boy? Was she depressed because there was some social activity coming up and she was the only girl without a date for it? In anger and disappointment she might have suddenly made up a boyfriend—a mysterious stranger. The whole confidence to Chris Stowe hinted of mystery, made her an object of interest to everyone. How soothing that would have been when she thought of past derision, however lightly it might have been thrust at her."

He looked from one to the other of them. Both faces

33

seemed to have taken on a blurred look, as though disappointment had dulled all vitality.

He said, more gently, "I'm not stating that as a fact, merely as a surmise—and after all," his grey gaze sought and held the younger man's, "what is your own story, but a surmise, based on a few words, a few out of the ordinary actions, a desire to escape blame for the girl's death, a pressing need to fasten blame somewhere else, far away from yourself?

"I told you, when we discussed the case of Oliver Harrap, that you can make a valid argument for many sides of every case, if you think hard enough. It's natural for you to take facts and turn them in a way that benefits yourself, but if you refuse to turn them this way and that way and see all the angles, clearly—all the stories that they could form, even if they didn't benefit you and rather, indeed, hurt you considerably, you're doing no one, not even yourselves, a service."

Shields was impatient now and eager to get back to the grey-walled office and the work waiting for him there, but when he thought of work there was the thought of Ann Aveyard to be faced, and the reflection that there were two weeks more before Mrs. Gold returned to the office. There would be two weeks with this girl at his side, facing him, staring at him with disappointed eyes, bringing up the subject of Robyn Calder, telling him how things were faring for Nigel Detrick and the other demonstrators.

He said sharply, angrily, "I'll see the police. I'll talk to them if they allow it. It may be possible to keep the case open for a little longer—at least until public opinion has ceased being so violent about the case. It may be the police have evidence that they haven't so far made public. I'll do that much for you," his gaze held Detrick's, "because I think you were in earnest and did your level best to see there was no violence or trouble of any sort. The fact that the very demonstration itself was an incitement on the part of others to become violent is something you appear to be unable to appreciate. No," his gesture was irritable

34

and dismissing, as was his frown, "I'm not entering into further debate. It's a waste of time. Accept that I'll see the police. It will be up to them whether they wish to talk to me or simply show me the door."

CHAPTER THREE

Seated in the small office with its strange smell compounded of decaying building overlaid with new cream paint, tobacco and humanity, Jefferson Shields was realising he was facing that most dangerous of witnesses—the person of authority who could see people only as types, never as individuals.

Where another, faced with an episode of student uproar, might say dispassionately, "This man bent and picked up a piece of handy rock and threw it at the building so that it hit the window glass," Sergeant Kevin Molloy would see the man as a type with which he was sadly familiar. He would reach into the filecard of his memory and say to himself, "Students behave in this fashion when they're misbehaving," and his evidence would be coloured by that fact so that he might say, "This student stopped and searched the ground until he found a sizeable chunk of rock, then he hefted it to the building and took careful aim so that the rock would strike and shatter the window."

The listener to the first statement would be left to make up his mind as to whether or not the glass smashing had been coolly and deliberately planned. The second statement gave them the answer and saved them the trouble of thinking and judging, and because it was human nature to slide from the responsibility of pinpointing blame, and because the man who gave the statement was invested with authority, his was the statement that would carry most weight.

Shields listened with that awareness of the speaker's character making him take each statement offered and strip it to the bare bones of fact before he considered it, while his gaze was fastened on the big man opposite, taking in the once burly frame that was now beginning to sag at shoulders and waist, so that the blue uniform seemed ill-fitting and untidy. The big square face had a childishly pink, just-scrubbed look about it, but the wide, thin-lipped, tight mouth and the jut of the jaw spoke of stubbornness anything but childish. The eyes were small and deep set and hazel, under brows that were still thick and dark, while the hair combed back from the smooth pink forehead was sparse and almost white.

Kevin Molloy said, and he spoke with conviction, "It was a punch started it. One of the men students threw a punch at a respectable old chap trying to get through the mob of them, and the chap toppled half way over on to somebody else and..."

Shields sighed. He asked, quite mildly, "How do you know the older man was respectable, and that it was a student who took the offensive?"

He saw the small eyes blink rapidly and the mouth tighten. He was sure that few people ever questioned the big sergeant's statements. There was a rasp of annoyance in the quick, "The old chap had all the marks of a business-man minding his own business. Good suit, briefcase, the whole appearance. D'you reckon on that type starting a brawl?"

Shields knew his irritation was part of the feeling of futility, his sense of wasting valuable time, but the room was too hot, too and the smell of decay trying to hide under new paintwork was growing stronger. He tried to keep the irritation from showing as he pointed out, "You can't type anyone into a neat little filecard. What type of a day was it? Hot? Was the crowd dense? Had the old man had a bad morning? Quarrelled with a client? His wife? Had he just escaped being run over by a bus that refused to stop at a pedestrian crossing for him to pass over? That," he pointed out regretfully, "seems to happen to me quite often." He stared into the blank, pink features and said gently, "Don't you think that heat, a bad morning, a narrow escape from traffic—any or all those things, might make even the most respectable of men lose his temper when faced with an obstructed footpath, so that he might—just might

37

—face it as assured possibility, Sergeant—lash out with his foot at one of the seated students, or at a leg that was in his pathway?

"And the student? You can't type them either, and did he really throw a punch? Were you close enough to see every movement? Couldn't it possibly be that if he was kicked, he thrust out an arm, a hand, to ward off further aggression, and isn't it possible—carrying that surmise further—that if the respectable-looking man had been off-balance from his kicking-out, that a shove should topple him off balance completely?"

He offered apologetically, "There are always several ways of looking at events. Unless you are standing right on top of them, and can view every movement taking place it is rarely possible to lay the blame squarely on anyone."

The gaze had narrowed, along with the tightening of the thin-lipped mouth. With his irritation flaring out in sudden temper, Jefferson Shields told him, "Don't immediately thrust me into a filecard labelled Demonstration-sympathiser, and label me with the vices of such. I've merely pointed out cold, hard facts." When the older man didn't speak he went on rapidly, "Let's look at it in this way—so far as you know the trouble began in one particular area, when for some reason unknown one student elbowed, thrust, shoved, at a passer-by, who toppled back on to others. What area was this? You've mentioned the footpath. Was the man going straight ahead, or moving past the fountain towards the building entrance?"

The tight mouth relaxed just enough to admit, "*From* the building. He was heading past the pavement, towards the roadway."

"Where were you yourself?"

"On the road. Urging those on it to shift themselves."

"So you would be facing one another?" At the nod of the white head, Shields asked, "What happened after the man toppled?"

For a minute he thought he was going to get no reply. The big sergeant sat still, hands linked on the desk top in front of him, gaze blank, then he said slowly, and it was obvious he had been groping for words that couldn't be criticised, or condemned, or corrected, "He seemed to sort of ... bounce? ... jerk? ... I can't get the right word, but he shot forward again. It'd be natural enough for those he fell on to jerk him back?" His gaze and voice challenged the other man, and when there was no comment he offered, "And he collided with a woman walking along the pavement from east to west. She squawked, and toppled and I had my view cut off. A few students on the road bounced up to see over the heads of the others and find out what was happening, and when I got past and could see it was just a push and shove and bash and brawl with women screaming and men yelling.

"From there on, we weren't concerned with rights or wrongs or anything but clearing the whole area as quick as possible." There was resignation in his dry, "From practice at it we've got the whole thing down to routine. First thing is to get the traffic moving. At all costs. If you don't some of them'll start a rush for a stalled car and start shaking it and toppling it, then the driver panics, poor bastard. He wants out and he's not let and usually he's hurt. Then when one car's over the road's blocked, there's a rush for other cars that can't get forwards or backwards. There's no end to it if you once let the traffic stall, so first thing is keep it moving at all costs. Next is clear the footway—bundle everyone on it into the building and pen them. You can sort them out later. The offices and lifts get locked at the first sign of trouble, so they're penned in hallways and on the stairs. It's just a case of nobbing them off one by one to the waggons and away."

Shields questioned, "Would you have described that morning as a routine job? Did something break your planned tactics for handling...?"

"No," the denial was prompt. "The road was cleared and the traffic moving with no trouble. We had the usual squawks from innocent bystanders who got herded into the building off the footpath, but that's routine too and it's surprising how well they take it. We sort them out as quick as possible—students to the waggon and others to me and the other senior men for an apology, and soothing of ruffled feathers and they're usually so damned relieved it's all over they simply say, 'That's all right,' and scoot for other regions."

"You sort them out?" Shields repeated slowly. "Students to the waggon and others ... so whether they've thrown punches or not, the bystanders are always considered innocent of wrongdoing and are let free? No," he added sharply, "I'm not criticising that point. Anyone caught up in a mêlée would strike out to protect themselves, and unless they had used some weapon..." He stopped, then suggested, "Any weapon would be promptly dropped, of course, once the crowds were ... as you put it, herded into the building. It would be impossible to state that anyone in particular had ever possessed it. It would be simple flotsam of the riot. What weapons were found that day?"

"Oddly enough, only two. That's a bit of a record. We've picked up some beauties—home-made jobs that're enough to raise your hair. This time all we collected was a chair leg and a hammer."

"Nothing at all that could have been the weapon that killed Robyn Calder?"

The pink face was creased and ugly with a frown. "No, but we had a look in the fountain basin. You can see what we got if you like. There was rubbish galore in it, along with coins—you ever wondered why folks've got to throw coins in any bit of water they come across?—and a couple of keys and stuff like that, along with a steel rod that might've been cut off a curtain rod some time, and a short length of copper water piping." He shook his head. "The doctors say 'possible' to the latter, but it'd hit the bottom and it was all covered with muck, and where's the clue in a bit of water piping anyway? I reckon if you were bashing your way through the mob you'd hold on to what you had anyway—he wasn't to know he'd killed the girl, was he? So he'd hold..."

"Unless it was deliberate. Unless it was murder—planned murder. Unless someone went, deliberately armed, deliberately intent on killing her."

Idly he watched the shock ride over Molloy's features, rippling them inch by inch, reddening them, rounding the eyes and parting the tight line of lips. The deep voice rasped out angrily, "What're you getting at?"

"It has been pointed out to me that the safest place to kill someone is in the middle of a riot," Jefferson Shields confided. "To dress as a rioting student, to carry a placard espousing a cause, is a disguise available to any man—or woman; to kill—not to shove or to thrust, or to protect oneself or shield oneself—but to deliberately strike with the intention of killing, would be comparatively simple, also. Others involved would be intent on themselves, their own safety, their own aggressors, their own property and friends, and how simple to slip away, with no problems of disposing of the body after death."

He waited till Molloy had digested that, and was about to speak, then without giving him time, he began to speak himself, and told the big sergeant of the interruption to the girl's usual placid way of living in that last week. He mentioned the conversation with the second girl and brought forward the idea that Nigel Detrick had suggested —that she had been involved with a married man who was tiring of her while she had been pressing for continuance and some more permanent form of relationship.

When he finished Molloy sat silent, then he laughed. His big sagging body shook and swayed. The laughter roared, the sound bouncing back at Shields from the newly painted cream walls of the small office, battering at him, irritating him so that his own mouth tightened and he looked with real displeasure at the reddened, laughing face opposite.

Then abruptly the sergeant was serious again. He said flatly, "You don't swallow that, so don't give me that line. They're catching at straws to shift the blame off themselves. You reckon we're going to waste time on that sort of line? Oh no," it was a long drawn sound of protest as the younger man was about to speak, "don't go labouring it. I grant you that sort of story happens and it'll go on happening till the world blows up or we all give up sex,

41

and I grant you, doing a killing during a riot is possible, and maybe for all I know, it's happened somewhere in the world and some chap's got away with it and is laughing about it right now but in this case ... no." The word was flat and final and definite.

"Before you start arguing again," he went on, in that same final voice, "I'm going to tell you something that gives a lie to this Detrick and his talk of peace and turning the other cheek. He's dreamed up a good idea to try and turn everyone's attention off himself and the rest of them who started the riot, but it won't wash. They were armed all right, or some of them were, and who of them's going to admit to it now, or ever? Not one of them. You know it as well as I do, and whatever weapons they had they dropped quick smart.

"They were all over that building—on every floor sure, the offices were closed and locked against them, but the halls were freeways. There were closets and there were rubbish bins and god knows what all over the place. D'you reckon any of them were going to be hauled off to the waggons clutching their chair legs and bits of pipe and all the rest? They dropped them, of course, out of sight and we were too busy to start hunting right then, but when the air cleared—when we started to look for weapons—don't you reckon that by then the ones who'd got clear hadn't sneaked in and skimmed everything that could be called a weapon and brought into court against the others, right out of the place?

"You needn't pull a face or argue that point either. They'd only need to put on a decent suit, grab a case and walk in whistling. People would be back in the offices making up for lost time. They'd rake the rubbish bins, slip any weapons into their cases and walk out, still whistling, and I'll tell you flatly that's what usually happens, because if we can charge any of them with carrying a deadly weapon they've had it."

Shields asked, in real shock, "You actually saw them using ... weapons of some sort ... against each other? You..."

"No. I've told you what I saw. After that I was too busy sweeping the road and footpath clear, but they were armed all right. Look," he leaned forward, his voice less rasping in its earnestness, "it's all very nice and easy to talk about peaceful demonstrations and not hitting back and all the rest, but when it comes to the point—when you're faced with someone who's intending to put his bunched fist in your face, it's a damn sight different.

"A lot of those youngsters were mere kids. A lot were girls. It's all very well to talk of a search of everyone, but d'you reckon they stripped them all—girls and all? And when one was searched where'd they go? They'd be milling around with no eyes watching every movement. You can bet your life, some of them were scared stiff of what they might face and while they wouldn't have the faintest intention of starting a brawl theirselves, defence'd be a different matter. They'd reason that way, and you know it. Especially a girl would.

"Who searched them anyway? And how'd they make sure everyone—every last one—was searched? There's always the ones who tag along at the last minute—who suddenly join in at the tail end or half way down the line—anywhere they see a march and decide they ought to be in on it.

"It's just being ostrich-like to say they couldn't have had weapons. If Detrick honestly believes what he's claiming he's simply hiding his head from facts, and you know it as well as I do." The red face was thrust forward in sudden derision. "I'm no ostrich. Are you?"

"No," Shields admitted, "and it is a point I had already considered, especially in relation to the fact that at one previous demonstration there was violence so great that one girl at least—Robyn Calder in particular—fled from the scene."

"All right, so we're getting somewhere." The grin was triumphant as he leaned back, opening a drawer, pulling a folder from it and opening it, thrusting it across the desk at the other man. "You look at that. Look at it hard. Then see why I busted my breath laughing at talk of

43

murder. You look. Look hard."

Shields wasn't listening, though the rasp of voice went on pounding at his ears. He was staring down at the glossy photograph. There were a circle of faces, some blurred, some clear, and a girl, with long disordered hair, half turned towards the camera. Her right hand was raised. The fist was clenched, holding tightly to something dark and slender and rounded. The mouth was parted, the eyes wide and startled.

Molloy said, and the words came loudly, triumphantly, "That's Robyn Calder. Taken just before she died."

CHAPTER FOUR

This other office had the same smell of decay overlaid with new paint, the same bare, institutional look and the same outlook over the dingy back lane of the city, but the man who sat behind the scarred brown desk was totally different, younger, with receding jet black hair and surprisingly green eyes that seemed to burn from a face that was thin to the point of emaciation.

Inspector John Virtue's voice was soft, almost a caressing whisper, with a faint undertone of something that could have been distaste, displeasure, when he said, "It was pointless to have made an issue of it. Would it have helped, do you imagine? I suspect, very strongly, that it would have inflamed public opinion further. What was the point of us saying out loud, 'This girl, at least, was armed.'

"Mr. Shields, use reason. There are many—too many—people who see in these demonstrations a chance to be self-righteously aggressive themselves. Let us say out loud that this time we know some students had armed themselves and next time there will be another faction who arrive on the scene, armed, too, and armed with the self-righteous excuse they are there to protect property and innocent people and as they are aware the demonstrators go armed, they have naturally protected themselves, etc. etc." Gently he swivelled the black leather chair back and forth as he went on, "Possibly this was a case of self-defence. Possibly that very weapon she carried was used against her. Possibly she struck out at someone who appeared to threaten her with hurt and her hand was caught, the weapon wrenched away and then ... did that person think, 'I'll teach the little wretch a lesson,' and give her a good clout over the head?

"Frankly, we've been playing for time, a breathing space,

a cooling-off period. I'd hoped we might have got somewhere, been able to pinpoint blame, but..." he spread his hands wide, "we haven't, so we go into court next week, and then the whole sorry business gets further publicity, and we admit that this girl at least, was armed, if we have to, and public opinion is again at boiling point..." His hand bunched and banged down sharply on the arm of the chair. "I'd do away with the inquest if it were possible. What good is it going to do? We know she died. We know what killed her. We know where it happened. And nothing more. Not a thing more.

"But the public gets a treat." The face and soft voice were soured with bitterness. "It will condemn the wretched girl and the rest of the demonstrators, and parade its self-righteous feelings and possibly the University will remove Detrick, and next time there's a demonstration of any sort there'll be another faction on the sidelines, armed and waiting."

He demanded, "What made you come to us?"

Almost apologetically Jefferson Shields explained, his gaze still fixed on the glossy photograph on the desk.

John Virtue didn't laugh as the sergeant had done. He remained silent for a little, then he said shortly, "I can tell you one fact—the medical evidence makes it plain she'd never been sleeping around with anyone. That makes nonsense of any hint she'd been having trouble with a man who'd tired of her. The story—*if* true," his brows went up in enquiry, but Shields made no comment and the soft voice went on, "if true, it could be and certainly sounds as though it might be likely, that she intended to set up the old love-in-the-afternoon-while-the-flat-mate's-away routine." His thin shoulders moved in a dismissing shrug, "Does that concern us—and her death? Tell me why it should."

Jefferson Shields agreed, "It doesn't, of course. Detrick has made a lot—or rather, he made a great deal to me of the point—that the man has remained a mystery. I don't know if he is playing what Sergeant Molloy would call an ostrich act, or whether he honestly cannot see the reason

46

for it, but if the man were married, he would certainly not reveal himself as the girl's intended lover. Certainly he would never have tried to gatecrash a funeral that was a private affair, by invitation only."

"There!" Virtue's soft exclamation was triumphant.

"You know yourself it's nonsense—pointless, so far as we're concerned here. Is Detrick meaning to bring that tale into court?" He warned, "Advise him that Calder is likely to cut up rough. He's very high on moral values, with a great sense of rectitude in himself and in the girl. He's certain to come out fighting if the girl's reputation gets a hint of blackening like that. Take my word for it and make sure Detrick doesn't try to make trouble."

Jefferson Shields looked up. He asked. "Was Calder aware she was taking part in these demonstrations?"

"Oh yes. So he says. Says that if the girl's conscience told her she was morally right in supporting these causes it was her own concern, even if he himself might disagree. He tells us she always discussed the causes with him before she took part. There was never more than amicable disagreement between them about it. She made her point, he made his. He says, quite rightly, that she had to learn to stand on her own feet and think for herself some time.

"That business of her leaving home. We knew about that. Calder mentioned it himself, though as another fact about her level-headedness. According to him she'd discussed the idea with him. He'd told her she'd have to make up her own mind without help from outsiders, then if things went wrong she could blame no one but herself. A simple enough explanation, isn't it, of that last week of alternate up and down moods?"

The other man didn't answer. He was still gazing at the photograph on the desk. He asked, "Who is Calder? Apart from being the dead girl's father? What..."

"He's her uncle, actually." As Shields looked up sharply the other man nodded. "No secret. Daughter of his brother. The marriage broke up when she was an infant and Calder and his wife brought her up as their own. She always called them mother and father—saved explanations to outsiders.

He's a member of the parking police." With a sudden grin he added, "I've always thought a high moralistic streak must run through a man before he can book another poor devil for overstaying a parking meter five minutes! No, seriously, Shields, he's a mild, inoffensive chap—good war record—good citizen, good father. He's very cut up about losing the girl." Again he warned, "Don't let Detrick try that murder talk in court at the inquest."

He suddenly shot out, "You've given no more credence to it than I did. Why did you really come to us?"

Jefferson Shields hesitated, then apologetically spoke of Ann Aveyard, and this time the Inspector laughed outright.

He admitted, abruptly sobering, "I'm sorry for the kids you know. Admittedly, they're a pain in the neck to us here, and I'd sometimes like to put my boot in their backsides —and don't quote me on that, for God's sake, but occasionally I've looked at their pathetic scraps of placards and I know damn well they're right and officialdom's wrong about something and there's been once at least when I've thought to myself that if I had a few more guts and a few less years I'd sit down on the road along with them." He laughed, shook his head, "No, they go the wrong way about it and the whole set-up's open to too many abuses by other people—and worst of all, from our point of view, the police inevitably get pictured in a bad light.

"Look at this last set-up. The police got no sympathy, yet one man finished with a broken finger, one has an injured back from lugging those kids off the road and everyone finished with bruises and cuts—but they're regarded as something close to monsters. If we'd done nothing—can you picture it?" He closed his eyes as though the mental vision was unbearable. "The traffic stalled, fights everywhere, property damaged and innocent people hurt. If we'd stood by and let that happen we'd have been monsters more-so. We can't win, can we?"

Shields suggested bluntly, "I should imagine Molloy as the wrong man for the job. To put it plainly he has too many preconceived prejudices—he would be unable to visualise a student behaving in any fashion except one. By-standers behave in another fashion and never step out of that fashion, either."

The dark brows went up. The retort was icy, angry, "The press and the public judge, too. It's essential to have a man who's experienced at handling riots, who can be trusted not to panic, to waver, to hesitate. Molloy's the man I'd choose to have behind me in any riot."

With the softness back in his voice he asked, "You're especially interested in something in that photo. What?"

"The faces. Two women. Two men. Who took the photo?"

"A press man. He handed it to us. We haven't released it for publication. He co-operated and kept quiet."

"So you've put a name to him. What about the others?"

"Yes. One came forward of her own accord." His finger pointed. "The middle-aged woman. The girl we found in a nearby office. One of the men was working on a PMG job," his finger jabbed again. "The work had to stop when the students arrived. He was hanging around waiting for it to be over, and got swept up in the riot. Funnily enough the woman knew the other man as her insurance agent. Small world, hmm?"

He offered, "You can read their statements. They aren't helpful. She was alive then, and when the photo was taken everyone who was in it was startled and upset. They didn't want to be involved or have their names in the press or even the photo. The photographer was abused by the PMG chap. He fled, with the other man after him, arguing. The others turned away and struggled through the crowds too. None of them saw the girl again. She looks—would you call it frightened?"

For a long time Jefferson Shields went on gazing at the pictured face. "I think so," he agreed finally. "And that would account for her bringing the weapon into the open. What other photos were taken?"

"Very few. None helpful. You can see them. Too many cameras have been broken other times for the press to want to move in close-to now. Anyway, to put it cynically, photo one riot and you've got them all."

Jefferson Shields offered, "Once before she was frightened. Badly shocked, according to Detrick. She tried finding sanctuary in nearby buildings and shops and offices. Nobody would let her in."

"They wouldn't. As soon as we're sure where a demonstration is heading we try alerting everyone—especially the most vulnerable—the banks, the jewellery stores, places like that. It's not only against a rioting mob getting in. It's the dread of my life that organised crime's going to move in. That's what I meant by the demonstrations leading to abuses. I have nightmares about organised crime running these demonstrations to suit themselves, picking the site and the time, and then ... violence, full-scale robbery, possibly death.

"As it is, the demonstrations are stage-managed—half of them at any rate. Oh yes," he nodded to the other man's quick up-glance of surprise. "You go to these people and tell them your cause and they organise it—the march and the marchers and the speeches—the whole lot. No," he shook his head impatiently, "it's nothing we can legally stop. It's not a criminal activity. They're perfectly open about it, and they claim they preach non-violence and are actually helping us keeping order. Two men run it," his reflective gaze was on the opposite wall. "One's an acknowledged Communist. He appeals to the left faction. The other appeals to another type. Both are young, seemingly earnest and apparently honest. It's run from a place called The Thought Club—a coffee-bar, meeting place for what they call Thinkers—in other words, anyone who can spare a thought for the world's problems."

Cynicism tightened his voice when he went on, "I said they were seemingly earnest, apparently honest. If you really want a problem to solve, you could try telling me yes or no to that.

"I've been there myself and spoken to them. I've put men in—some as obvious police, some as apparent Thinkers. I still don't know. All I know is I've a nasty taste in my mouth and nasty thoughts about it all, because nearly every time there's a wild demonstration, there's a strike somewhere else in the state. It's not confined to this state—it happens in the lot of them. The big cities have a demonstration and somewhere else there's a strike. It's always senseless, always without warning and always at a time to cause the most loss in terms of manpower, and contracts and inconvenience to the country in general.

"The public doesn't notice. The riots in the big cities are the news they want to read about, so that hits the front pages. The wild-cat strikes are dismissed with a few brief paragraphs in some inside page.

"It's too much of a coincidence. Some time, visit this Thought Club for me. Speak to those men—Athol Lesie and Rex Bratton. Come back and tell me what you think of them—of the whole set-up there."

"Are they in your nightmares?" Shields enquired. "Do you see them organising crime...?"

"No-o. At least ... well we could get them for crime perhaps if it were that. No, there's something, but I'd plump for the political angle." He said without emotion, "They're a thoroughly detestable pair of apparently pleasant men. Make what you can of that contradiction."

He shook his dark head and said decisively, "My nightmares about crime don't contain them at all."

"Tell me—has there ever been crime—a big-scale robbery—a bank hold-up, while...?"

"No. Not yet. There's car stealing, though. Could be organised on a big scale or be by several operators. Everyone's attention is on the demonstration area, so it leaves a clear field for car thieves in other places. There's plenty of petty crime. Adds up to quite a sum. You see, when these shows start the lower floor offices of a building and the lifts are all locked. Rioters can't get to the upper floors simply because everyone from the upper offices is milling out into the corridors, to block the stairways and hang out the windows and view the fun. It's an excuse to stop work and they never seem to think of locking the offices behind them, unless there are some obvious valuables about.

"Everyone rushes to one side of the building and mills around. While that's happening one, or two, or perhaps

51

more, see an opportunity. It's spur-of-the-moment crime—one man could go through all the offices on several floors, or two or more people might get the same idea, but look at it from the petty thieving point of view for a minute. Here are offices deserted and no one looking and girls leave their purses in desk drawers. It doesn't take long to whisk open desk and purse. A few dollars here, a few more there, a bit of jewellery perhaps—and it can add up to a nice little haul."

He brushed the question aside with an impatient, "But it's petty stuff. Occasionally we actually nail a prosecution, but it's rare. It's not that I'm worried about and frankly it's putting temptation in people's way to leave the offices open to theft that way.

"It's a big crime..." His voice trailed off. "And those two—Athol Lesie and Rex Bratton." He urged again, hopefully now, "Go and talk to them." He pressed, "You might even stumble on the name of the chap—the stranger—young Robyn Calder met that other demonstration day."

Abruptly he laughed again. He urged, "Tell your blessed Ann Aveyard that you're hanging round the Thought Club, making enquiries. It will keep her off your back and maybe you'll put a finger on something I've missed." The black leather chair stopped swivelling. He asked, in a brisker voice, "Do you really want to wade through the statements of those four in the photo, and the press man?"

Jefferson Shields hesitated, then nodded. "I may as well," he agreed, and there was faint apology in his voice, a faint apology in his manner that the other man dismissed with a crisp, "As you like then."

CHAPTER FIVE

The day had begun badly for Kate Hough. The clock had fooled her. She had completely forgotten that in the last few days it had taken to being unreliable, so that she arrived at the bus stop to see the green rear of the bus vanishing round the corner.

She stood there, pink faced from exertion and temper, feeling the good town shoes pinching her plump feet and the new corsets gripping her far from trim waist in an embrace that cut off her breath.

For one minute she was tempted to simply go home, kick off the offending shoes and ease out of the corsets and forget about shopping, but as quickly as the idea had come she forgot about it, because she was seeing Greta's young face and hearing her voice commanding, "You get a new dress, mum, before Saturday. If you turn up wearing your old black lace *again* I'm going to die—just *die*."

Terrible, the intensity of sixteen, Kate reflected, half in irritation, half in amusement, but she had to admit that Greta was right. The old black lace had seen too many outings and socials and parents' nights altogether.

That meant town because the local shops didn't stock what they called outsizes. Kate referred to it, when she had to, as being awkwardly built. Her blue eyes would open in pained innocence and she would say, as though the fact puzzled her, "I'm just an awkward size to fit, short and with a fuller figure than's strictly fashionable."

Town meant the bus, or taking the car. She debated which was the worse, waiting an hour for the next bus, which meant going home and sitting there, stiff as a board in the new corsets, till it was time to go to the corner again, or taking the car in and trying to find a parking spot without risk of coming back and finding a parking ticket on the windscreen.

Reluctantly she decided against the bus. Half trotting, she went back to the house and fetched the car keys and in another two minutes the little blue car was edging on to the road and turning towards the city.

Kate regretted it, of course, just as she had expected to, before she'd even passed the inner suburbs. It was hot, and all the smells of too-close living and tannery factories and foreign cooking seemed enclosed between the brick walls of the narrow streets that huddled close to the city. By the time she saw the clock tower of Central Railway her head was aching and her eyes watered from the glare, and when she finally found a vacant parking meter and had the car safely parked she felt exhausted, and as close to real blazing temper as her usually placid nature permitted.

It was hardly soothing, when she came out of one of the department stores, after being told her awkward figure had grown, just in the space of a couple of months, even too awkward for their styles, to find herself facing the uniformed bulk of a young policeman and hear him say, "I wouldn't go *that* way, if I were you, madam. There's a student demonstration coming up that way."

"Students!" All the irritation of the morning, her sore feet and her pinched waist and the knowledge she had gained six pounds in two months, exploded in the burst of sound from Kate's lips, and in her furious glare. Even the young policeman took a step backwards in alarm. At another time she might have burst out laughing and reflected on the joke of being with the family in the evening and describing the scene to them and boasting she'd frightened a six feet copper, but she was simply too angry.

Demonstration or not she intended to cross the road and reach the department stores further down. Trotting again, just catching the Walk sign at the pedestrian crossing in her hurry, she went across the road to the opposite footpath and started down it.

She was sorry of course. Just as she had been about bringing the car in, because before she had realised what was

54

happening she seemed to be part of a crowd pressing and jostling, and everywhere she looked there was scowling faces and angry mutters.

She said in alarm to an angry male face, "What is it?" though she knew, remembering the young policeman and his warning.

The face mouthed at her, "Pacifists!" and then bent to roar the information into her ear, with the addition, "*Bloody* pacifists, madam!"

Startled and confused by both roar and the crowd she pressed back and the crowd opened, so that she nearly fell, then it engulfed her again, jostled and pushed her and spewed her out, shaken and really frightened, into sight of a fountain.

She saw a rainbow in the water, which surprised her. Her fright was so great she was surprised she could take in anything, then a voice said, "Look out!" and she was pushed aside. She tried to turn, to see who it was, and then she saw the girl and her attention was caught in shocked amazement, because the child—surely not older than Greta, Kate thought in honest distress—was armed with something that looked unpleasantly like a short iron bar.

It wasn't that fact that held her, but the thought that popped into her head, the realisation that the girl was just as frightened as Kate herself—that the reddened cheeks and open mouth didn't speak of viciousness, but sheer fright, and the realisation that the girl was rushing towards Kate and others near her and mouthing, unheard over the noise, a desperate cry, "Let me out!"

She wondered if others saw it, too and understood, because for a moment there was a clear space about the girl, and then a flash of light, that made Kate cry out in alarm. It took her a few seconds to realise that someone had photographed the scene, and then she cried out herself in dismay and panic. The thought of herself in the papers, for all the neighbours to see and talk about—in connection with a riot, and maybe her name too, published for everyone's eyes to note, was thoroughly shocking.

Like the girl, she was suddenly crying, "Let me out!"

and turning back the way she had come, pushing and shoving, violently. She saw another woman thrust back against the wall by one shove, dealt by herself, and while she was sickened and astounded that she could behave like that, she went on fighting at everyone who stood in her path.

The crowd spewed her out again. She stood on the pavement staring at milling bodies and a surging wave of police and felt so sick she nearly burst into tears. She could see the other woman again—mouth open and eyes terrified—crashing back against the wall, and the tears actually welled into her blue eyes, at the knowledge that she, Kate Hough, could have been, in those few minutes, turned into an uncivilised savage whose one instinct was self-preservation, at all costs, at whatever damage to anyone else.

Then the thought was gone. Still staring at others spewed out like herself, who wandered past her, all she could think about was the car and what Jim was going to say if anything happened to it. She had to get back to it, fast, she told herself, and get it out of the city, right away from all the violence, that might at any minute spread out and down to the area where she had left the car.

Hurrying, staggering a little from past shock and shakiness, she turned her back on the struggling crowd and walked away. She didn't look back.

.　　.　　.

For Judy Moon the day dawned excitedly, because she was starting a new job. She expected a lot from it, not only in terms of cash and things to buy with it, but in what was more important still to her—men.

The old job had been good enough. She'd told the family that when they'd objected to her leaving, but she had long ago found out all there was to be known about the men she met there, had assessed them all and found them all lacking in what she termed desirability—and that, to Judy, meant push and drive, the ability to get on and make a lot of money and more, to see that Judy Moon was exactly the sort of wife a man like that needed.

So she was excited, and by eleven o'clock had found disappointment. Her work was going to be exclusively with women, under a sour-faced supervisor who appeared to regard herself as a kind of chastity belt on office life. Life for Judy Moon, the woman had made it plain within an hour, was going to be a round of copy typing in the main office, with occasional sorties into the world outside to post mail and buy staff lunches.

It was a relief when she was sent off to the post office with a parcel for registration. Once outside the office door, in the corridor, Judy let out a long-pent breath, and childishly poked out her tongue at the closed door, as a relief to her feelings, as derision to the cold voice tolling her departure with, "You have exactly fifteen minutes, Miss Moon, to register the parcel and return. I will require a full explanation of any delay. See that I do not have to ask for it."

"Cripes!" she ejaculated softly, and repeated it. She went down the corridor wondering if they'd pay her if she handed in her resignation when she went back. She wondered, giggling aloud at the thought, if they'd ask her for a reason and what they'd say if she gave back, "I'm not a machine. I can't take exactly fifteen minutes to post a parcel, or ten minutes to type one page, or three minutes to go to the loo and pee."

She was still laughing when she went towards the building's main door and out on to the street. The sunshine was a relief after the chill cloistered life of the office upstairs. She stood for a minute revelling in it, poking derision at chastity-belt's timetable. She went on standing, forgetting timetables completely, as she saw the crowd.

Interested, she edged forwards to see what was on the placards the seated groups were holding. She saw the ranked lines of uniformed police on the roadway, saw one of them speaking to the group who were seated on the road.

There was no fright or awareness of danger in her as she kept edging forward in interest and a sudden thought that here was an excuse ready-made for her late return to the chill office. Even old chastity-belt wouldn't be able to say a word if Judy Moon stood up and said, "Didn't you see the fun and games down there? There were crowds all over the pavement and road and I couldn't get past, or even back, because my way was blocked."

She glanced over her shoulder to see if that was true, because for all she knew the woman upstairs might even have been gazing out the window right then. It was because of that she didn't see the first punch, the first hint of danger. One minute there was only interest and a pleasurable excitement, the next she was really frightened, and she couldn't go back—couldn't do anything but allow herself to be swept away in the surge of bodies pressing and milling and yelling and jostling about her.

She heard her own voice cry out, and felt the parcel torn from her hands. She didn't try to resist. She let it fall. Her resistance and strength was kept for trying to push backwards, but it was useless. She was pushed forwards, then sideways. In panic she began striking out. Faces swam into view, were thrust at and receded, mouthing at her in anger and fright, then abruptly she was clear, close to the fountain. She was thrust against a plump woman. Judy clutched at her, to remain upright. The woman didn't seem to notice her. She was staring at someone. She looked shocked and bewildered and Judy's own glance whipped sideways.

She said aloud, "Cripes!" and instinctively ducked, fearing the girl in the jeans and jacket, with the upraised hand holding the bar, would hit out at herself, but the girl didn't seem to notice her.

There was a sudden flash. Judy cried out again, frantic now, "Cripes!" and put up an arm, trying to shield her face from further photos.

Her one thought was to get away, her one hope that the photo hadn't shown herself, or at least not so clearly that anyone who knew her would recognise it.

She was telling herself, as she elbowed and shoved and pushed her way back through the crowd, that if anyone did she might get called as a witness. She didn't want to be. She didn't want it suggested she had something to do with the riot, either and someone might. She was nearly crying when she was finally free of the crowd again and astonished, she fought free to find herself against the same plump woman as before.

The woman was muttering to herself in little squeaking, shocked sounds that didn't make words. Judy watched her, while leaning against the nearest wall, trying to get back her breath, abruptly remembering the fallen parcel and wondering what was going to be said about it.

She saw it then. Amazingly it was on the fringe of the crowd. She was sure it was the one—that it was hers, but she didn't dare go back to try and reach it for fear the crowd surged back and engulfed her again.

She waited, simply leaning against the wall, hoping the row would stop as quickly as it had started. No one was paying any attention to the parcel. The mob still swayed and jostled and every few seconds another body was spewed forth and went past her, eyes glazed, lips working and twitching with shock. All of them were ordinary people. None of them were students. None were armed, as the girl by the fountain had been.

Finally it was over, but the parcel had completely vanished. She went slowly back to the office. She had meant to make herself the centre of attention with her story.

Instead she simply stood inside the doorway and burst into noisy tears.

.   .   .

For John McCulloch the day began like any other working day, taking the PMG repair van where she was needed, and getting down to the work of checking wires and cables, and finding out what was wrong.

After twenty years in the same job he was inured to the stickybeaks and wisecracks and even to the few who stopped and stared at him and began to ply him with earnest questions. He ignored the first types and treated the latter with an outward courtesy that gave no hint he was mentally blasting them for wasting precious time.

It was simply an annoying interruption to his day when the policeman stopped and advised him to pack up.

"Student demonstration?" McCulloch thought that over, his lean face grimacing. "I'd give them a demonstration —of bottom whacking—if I'd my way."

The other grinned. He intoned, "It is showing the maturity of the individual in recognising the minority claims of a democratic society." Derisively he added, "That's what I got told by one of the last mob, so if you don't want the minority of a democratic society to make a mess of your job you'd best pack up."

Worriedly McCulloch demanded, "You reckon on them taking long?"

A shrug was his only answer. For a minute he stood watching the blue-uniformed back moving away, then resignedly he began to pack up, one eye cocked for signs of a march.

It came faster than he had expected. He turned the lock on the van, to see the crowd dropping, settling themselves over the footpaths and roadways. He saw one youth solemnly dropping coins into the three nearest meters and reluctantly grinned, because the business had been so neatly stage-managed—the meters had been occupied up to then by cars that had swung out in unison just as the marchers approached.

He saw a policeman go forward to argue with the coin-dropper. The youth was laughing, pointing out, evidently, that he had dropped in the required coins and had a right to the meter space.

Some of the crowd laughed. The policeman turned, anger in the taut lines of his body and face.

"Easy, mate," McCulloch softly admonished from his place on the outskirts, "Easy does it. Don't lose your cool now."

As though he had heard, the other man turned sharply away again, going back to join the main body of blue-uniformed police.

There was an air of waiting about everyone—even McCulloch, and then suddenly the waiting and the peace was gone. He didn't see what happened to start it—only that in a fraction of a second people were fighting. He saw an elderly woman pushed to the ground and it was instinctive in McCulloch to rush forward, to try and help. The crowd seemed to spread out and surround him and the woman and thrust them forward. The woman was wrenched away from him and he never saw her again or bothered about her, because his mind was centred on taking care of himself and fighting free.

It was perhaps only a couple of minutes—perhaps longer —that he found himself near the fountain, and right in front of a girl—a student it had to be, he told himself— and she was coming at him, her hand up and something ugly and shocking in it. It looked like an iron bar. Instinctively he stepped back, as a light flashed and McCulloch's gaze slid sharply sideways. Rage and panic welled up in him. He jumped sideways, crashing against the photographer, snarling at him, "Quit that!"

The man wrenched free, jostling and pushing his way against the crowd, McCulloch after him, furiously angry, demanding he hand over the camera, that he hand over the print, that he'd sue him if he published the photo, knowing all the time that he raged that he was behaving like a complete fool, but unable to stop himself.

He lost the other man in the crowd and with the loss his rage died. Somewhere or other he had taken a blow on the temple. The bruise was beginning to throb and burn. He could think only of that as he began to fight, furiously, not caring now whom he hurt, just so long as he was free and out of the trouble-spot.

Just as quickly as he'd tumbled into trouble, he was out of it, gasping, staggering, shaking with the shock. He stood on the edge of the pavement, taking in great gulps of air, staring stupidly at the fighting crowd, watching people stagger out of it, as shaken and shocked as himself.

None was armed. All of them were ordinary people— women who'd been shopping, men who'd been going about business affairs.

Then abruptly, still watching the crowd, he remembered

the repair van. He told himself to move, fast, to get it away and out of danger, reminding himself that if the crowd shifted back an official van of any sort was the first thing a mob might go for and try to destroy, but even with his mind urging him to move and get it out of danger, he couldn't do more than drag himself along the footpath.

.   .   .

For Patrick Frawley the morning was the same old drag as usual—up and shake out the cornflakes and shave and shower and hope your shirt was dried overnight when you'd put it dripping over the bath, and wonder where your last pair of socks had hidden themselves and pick up your briefcase that made you look like a businessman even when there was nothing in it, and then outside and catch a bus and have your toes walked on by a sullen-faced woman who met your apology—and why apologise as though you had no right to put your feet where she could stand on them?—with a scowl and a look that said she felt worse than you and she meant you to know it and wasn't life hell?

Then you got to work and there was always someone to point out you were five minutes late and you blamed the transport department and got a ha-ha-tell-me-another and a warning that next time you lost five minutes pay as though you were owned lock stock and barrel nine to five, Mondays to Fridays, from here to eternity. The usual things went wrong, like finding your last ballpoint had run out of ink and the client you'd thought you'd enrolled in the fold had changed his mind and gone somewhere else and you had to write an explanation for head office, though how you were supposed to be able to set down the working of someone else's mind you didn't know, so you put down anything that sounded reasonable and wondered if head office was staffed with fools the way they accepted your stories without comment.

Then you made a show of looking at your appointment diary and thought to yourself, dear God, here's a chance to get away from Elwin's sniffles and the smell of cough medicine, and you say you're going out to keep an appointment, which fools nobody because they're all trying to think of an excuse to get out to coffee too, but you get away and then all of a sudden, the day turns completely different. There's a demonstration going on in the street outside and an officious policeman tells you to stay inside the building, won't you, sir, and keep the footpath clear and you're sick to death of being ordered about, so you tell him back you've an important appointment that won't wait on anyone so good morning to you, and you march out and the world goes bang.

It kept going bang—bang into his side and his back and his arms and legs and shoulders and even bang on his head, so that he started to bang back and because he had the briefcase the crowd parted and let him through. He found himself by the fountain with a couple of women to one side of him and a girl in front of him who seemed to want to give him a good bash.

He went to swing the briefcase in front of his head and face from her rush forwards, and found to his astonishment that he had only the handle left. He was staring at it stupidly when the photo was taken.

Because the briefcase had gone and he no longer had it to shield his face from photos either, he turned sharply away. The crowd had rushed forward again. He was caught in it and carried away and someone said, "Take that!" and smashed at his face. He smashed back and went on smashing at anything handy till he was suddenly out of it, standing on the fringe of it, staring over his shoulder in shocked disbelief that he had ever been part of it.

He didn't want to be caught up in an official grab and made to give evidence of any sort. Hastily, he turned. Quite unconscious of the absurd figure he cut he began to hurry along the street, still clutching the briefcase handle, his arm automatically swinging the briefcase that was no longer there.

CHAPTER SIX

There was a mild irritation in walking in to the outer office and finding Nigel Detrick there, his hands behind Ann's blonde head as they stood together, the girl's eyes gazing into his, her slim hands on the shoulder of his brown jacket.

He said only, with a chilling courtesy, as the two sprang apart, "Miss Aveyard ... my office please," and walked on past them, a thin grey-clad figure, grey head slightly thrust forwards as though his gaze was eager to fasten on the grey-walled sanctuary of his office beyond.

So there was anger in his first startled sight of the figure sitting there.

The girl rose when she heard him. She grinned at him, the wide smile revealing good teeth, and a dimple in one cheek. She might have been Ann's sister. There was the same long swinging blonde hair, the same too-brief skim of skirt, though hers was red, and the same square-framed, black-rimmed spectacles, but instead of Ann's neat, pin-tucked white blouse, this other girl had a white jersey under a hip-length black leather jacket.

She said without preamble, "I'm Chris Stowe, Mr. Shields," and the wide grin flashed again, expectant of welcome, of pleasure that she was there waiting for him.

The smile vanished when he went round behind the desk without speaking. He stood in front of his grey leather chair, slowly, with great deliberateness, because he was still fighting anger, fixing his spectacles on his nose. He looked up then—at the girl the other side of the desk, and behind her to the slimmer figure of Ann Aveyard, and beyond her again to the bulk of Nigel Detrick.

He wanted to say, "For heaven's sake, go away." He

wanted to ask, "Why did you come here?"

It was Ann who spoke. She took two steps forward, and her face and voice were both defiant when she said, "We wanted you to hear what Chris has to say. What Robyn told her. About that man—that stranger—that..."

"That man in the moon!" he silenced them brusquely and sat down.

He surveyed them, his hands linked on the desk over the piled papers that waited his attention. He said, with only weariness now, "You have taken up a great deal of my time. You have made me listen to a great many theories and suppositions and ideas. You have made me do things I didn't care to, and you have made me go to the police on your behalf. No," he held up a warning hand as Nigel moved, "don't interrupt, I have more to say. You have behaved remarkably like children expecting a magician to wave a hand and turn a black cat into a snow-white one.

"No, again, don't interrupt. I have been to the police. They are well aware of the fact Robyn Calder was contemplating leaving home. She had discussed it with her father. She was undecided what to do. One one hand she wished to widen her horizons. On the other, she dreaded the prospect of leaving the shelter and comfort of her known home. Those would be her thoughts, so her moods would swing from fear and withdrawal, to expectancy and pleasure, during that last week of her life.

"If there was a man who had entered her life—if indeed, that was not a story made on the spur of the moment to make her a mystery woman, a woman who was desired by someone unstated—whatever she contemplated in regard to their future, she had never had any sexual relationship with him, or any other man."

He saw stark disappointment in Detrick's face. He went on flatly, "The funeral was a private affair, by invitation only. If this man had ever contemplated making her his mistress, he would never have admitted it after her death. Even if there *was* a man in her life, nothing tells us that the matter wasn't one-sided. She had met a stranger Nothing would be the same for her, ever again. She stated—

was that wishful thinking, a hope, a dream, alone?—that nothing would be the same for him, either. We cannot know that was true. She might have met a man, certainly, and fallen in love and built foundations on that feeling that had no basis in reality. Girls have done so before this and will do so till eternity.

"Perhaps she might have dreamed that if she had more freedom, was more available, was not tied to home, to keeping her father company, she would seem more desirable to him and make more headway. Perhaps that was why she wished to have a home of her own.

'All that matters is that there was no man who had used her sexually, then tired of her, and murdered her because she was making demands he couldn't meet. That," his gaze fastened on the other man's face, he saw sullenness—anger and a flat despair, as he went on, "that was wishful thinking, a dream, a hope, on your part alone.

"I've read the statements of the people who saw her last. Not students. Not the man you mentioned, Mr. Detrick, but others later on. They saw her by the fountain, the place where she died, perhaps only seconds before she was killed.

"They cannot say more than that she was there; and that she was alone—and that she was armed." The statement came with flat finality.

"No!" The retort came explosively. Nigel Detrick took three strides across the grey carpet. His big, scarred hands came down flat on the desk top and his bearded face was thrust towards the older man. He said bitterly, "That's a damned lie, for a start." He swung round on the girl in the black jacket. "Isn't that a lie?" he demanded of her passionately.

Chris Stowe said gravely, almost gently, "He must have a basis for saying it—a proof, or he wouldn't have said it."

Jefferson Shields gave her a thoughtful glance. He reflected that Nigel Detrick, for all his bulk, for all the manual labour that had scarred his hands, and his air of authority, had still an innocence, a trust in the world, a belief in miracles that had made him grasp at the hope of

66

murder, that had made him thrust it hopefully forwards, just, as Shields had pointed out, like a child who was asking an adult magician to make a black cat white.

Ann, for all her efficiency, was the same, but this girl, in the black leather jacket, with her grave, thoughtful, deep voice and her steady scrutiny, though she was certainly younger than Nigel, possibly younger than Ann, was older than both of them. Here was a girl who had closed the door on the land of magic and magicians and black cats turning into white at the whisk of a hand and a magic word.

Although when he had first seen her there, when she had said in that expectant way, "I'm Chris Stowe," he had told himself that he wasn't going to waste time on her; had no intention of speaking to her or let her tell him anything, he knew now that he was going to talk to her; that he wanted to. For the sake of a nagging curiosity that was likely to be unsatisfied forever, as to how Robyn Calder died, he wanted to hear about that mention of the man— the stranger—who had come to Robyn's life.

He told them, "There was a photograph. It will almost certainly be—must be, I should imagine—brought into evidence at the inquest. It was taken by a photographer who freelances for various press agencies. I have gone over his statement. It tells nothing. It says that he was told of the demonstration and went to get photos if possible. He was caught up in the crowd. By the fountain he saw a girl and because she was newsworthy, because she was armed, because she was proof of aggression on the part of the students, he snapped her, and four others who stood close to her.

"Their statements are available, too, because all were found by the police. All were innocent bystanders, caught up in the crowd, spilled out together near the fountain. All saw Robyn Calder. All saw the weapon she carried, but because of that photo, because they didn't want to be involved, to have their names taken, they turned sharply away.

"They saw no one else near her. They saw no one come

67

out of the crowd who was behaving suspiciously, who was armed, who looked as though they knew they had killed.

"No one knows what happened after that. There is only that one fact that Robyn Calder was armed. Her hand was raised, in aggression. One bystander said that the girl was frightened, was crying to be let out of the crowd. Isn't it only too possible, as the police will suggest in court, that she struck out and her hand was caught, the weapon wrenched away and she in her turn was given a good crack with it, to teach her a lesson?"

Nigel straightened. There was only shock and bewilderment left in his face. The anger was gone and the defiance and hope, too.

He said, "She wasn't armed—when we left."

"How can you be sure?" Shields derided brusquely. "As the police say, did you strip everyone? Did you keep each one apart after searching, so they didn't disappear from sight, even for one moment? Did you make sure that some persons didn't join the march on its route, and hand out weapons to those who wanted them?"

While the younger man was still riding the shock of that, Shields demanded, "What do you know about this Thought Club? Did you ask them to master-mind this demonstration for you? Did they have the final say in the planning? Did ..."

Dusky red crept up under the sun-tanned skin. The big head was shaken violently. "That for a story! We had nothing to do with them. Oh, all right, I know full well they'll plan a demonstration, a march, a meeting, for you if you want it, and perhaps some people from there joined in along the route for all I know, but ... so far, mind you, as I know, they're helpful and they're straight and they certainly can organise, but this was only a small affair, it was ... spontaneous perhaps ... arranged out of discussions between two or three people here, three or four there, another couple somewhere else, each one saying to another, 'Look, I've heard these other chaps talking about this, too— how about seeing them and thrashing the matter out with them, too?' till finally all the groups were consolidated into one mass. Do you follow that?"

After a brief hesitation he went on, "The subject of a demonstration wasn't brought up for quite a while. First we discussed ways of helping Harry—comforts we might send him; letters, if the authorities permitted it, and we were anxious to find out if he could keep his studies up in there. Things like that. Then the talk got around to a petition to parliament. That was when we got down to tin-tacks. Someone else said that Canberra'd simply file the petition in some pigeon-hole and send us a lot of porridge about the matter having attention and thank you for your letter. The suggestion cropped up we present the petition in person and first we should get signatures from the general public, too. That was what the demonstration was about. We intended to have speeches there in front of the crowds and ask bystanders to give their signatures to the petition form we'd hand around.

"There was nothing that needed organising. It was strictly a friends-of-Oliver-Harrap affair. If the police are going to claim we asked the Thought Club to arrange a full-scale riot, with weapons handed out along the route, we'll..." He stopped, then said helplessly, "We'll be finished. The University will be forced to take some action. You do see that, don't you?"

"Yes. Do you mean this Thought Club advocates violence? According to the police ..."

"No! I've given you a false line!" The denial came swiftly and definitely. "I've never known them preach anything to do with violence—the reverse. What I meant is— if the police are going to make out this was a ... well, *professionally* organised business, they can go one step further and claim the arming of the crowd was arranged for, too." He asked anxiously, "Hasn't anyone an idea where she got the weapon? What was it anyway?"

"It looks like an iron bar. It's been described as that—as a short iron bar."

Detrick grimaced. All hope seemed to have gone out of him. His big body seemed slumped and sagging. He said helplessly, "It looks as though we've had it—all of us. The

69

University couldn't afford to let things slide. There's going to be hell to pay in the press when it comes out..." He looked up sharply, "Was anyone else armed?"

"I don't know. There are no reports of it, though a hammer and a chair leg were found, discarded, after the riot had stopped. I intended to see the press photographer and ask him, and see if there weren't some photos that were discarded as too blurred, or no use, either for the police or the press. He's not available, until later today."

He turned sharply to the silent girl in the chair across the desk. "Miss Stowe, were *you* armed?"

She said, looking at him fully, without defiance, as though saying aloud that she, at least, had nothing to hide, no shame in what had happened. "No. I never have been at any demonstration I've attended. I wouldn't touch that sort of business for anything. It's sheer madness."

"Even if you were frightened? Wouldn't you arm yourself if you were frightened you might be badly hurt without something, other than your hands, to protect yourself?"

"Not even then," she gave back definitely. "There's no end to that sort of thing—one blow gathers another in return. Besides, if it was a stronger person—if you're a woman and a man lashed out at you for example—and you were armed and hit at him he could easily overpower you just the same, and if you'd hurt him, made him lose control and his temper and his common sense, well..." she gave a little shrug, "you can guess the way events would go, for yourself. You think that's what happened to Robyn. The police think so, too." The same dejection as in the young man's voice showed in hers as she added, "So that's that."

Ann began, "But there must be something..." and Detrick whirled on her savagely, tight anger in his barked, "Quit! Just quit, right there! It's like he," a big hand jerked over his shoulder, "says—wishing won't make a black cat white."

Shields gave them a few minutes before he spoke again. He asked at last, turning to Chris Stowe, "I'd like to hear about that talk you had with Robyn Calder. No, no reason," he admitted apologetically, "except curiosity. I keep wondering whether her talk of a man was a lie, or the truth."

She seemed to be pondering that, sitting slackly in the grey chair, a slight frown above the black-rimmed glasses. Finally she said, "I'd have said it was the truth. I mean— you've said yourself that girls romance—make themselves appear mysterious and desirable. That's correct. At University especially I expect. If you've no dates, aren't in the full centre of things, you'd get a feel of inadequacy I should think, though I've never experienced it." There was no boasting in the statement, just a simple statement of fact.

Shields suggested, "There was some mockery, at least, in the fact that men wanting to drop a girl told her to go and play chess with her father—a reference to Robyn Calder who spent her evenings doing that instead of dating?"

For the first time she hesitated and appeared uncomfortable, then she said, "Cruelty is a hard thing to define, Mr. Shields. To an outsider that might appear to be worse than it was. I wouldn't call it mockery. A lot of the men were big-brotherish, or do I mean good mates? ... they were friendly with her on a strictly unisex level. I mean there was nothing in the slightest degree like romantic attraction, but she wasn't either disliked or a person who was merely barely tolerated.

"She was simply a rather introverted person who was a good deal younger than the rest of us on certain points— dating for one. When the men said that to a girl—'Go and play chess with your dad'—I honestly think most of them meant, 'What's good enough for Robyn is good enough for you, so stop pestering me—Robyn gets pleasure out of that, why can't you occasionally do it instead of always wanting me to parade you round town?' Does that give you a new slant on it?" she asked hopefully.

"Perhaps, but did Robyn Calder herself see it from that point of view? Or did she take it for mockery?"

Her colour deepened. "I don't know," she admitted.

"Leave the point then," he suggested. "Just tell me what she said to you that day. How did the conversation begin in the first place? There's been some mention that she was close to tears when she was speaking to you. Had there been some event that had upset her just previously to your talk?"

"No. She didn't appear ... weepy, wanting a shoulder to cry on. She seemed excited, apprehensive—something like that. There *was* a hint of mystery in what she said, in her manner—a sort of 'There are things I could tell you that would open your eyes if you only knew them' manner about it, and frankly, it did leave me with the impression she'd become involved with a man who was going to make a fool of her."

"Did you ... preach ... at her? Try to warn her ... ?"

"Good lord, no!" She sounded astonished. "It was none of my business what she did. Besides, preaching usually makes the listener run in the very direction you're preaching against!" The dimple showed in her cheeks again, as she laughed.

Jefferson Shields nodded. He asked again, "How did the talk start?"

"She'd asked me—before that—the previous day I think —if I'd like to flat-mate with her, and I'd said no. Definitely not. I was too comfortable as I was. I'm boarding with my brother and his wife in the suburbs. My home's in the country," she explained. "I get free board and lodging for the sake of baby-sitting the kids. It means I can spend my living allowance on other things. I told her that, but offered to ask around for her.

"So, that day of our talk, she cornered me and asked if I'd gotten anywhere, and I had to admit no. I pointed out it was a bit late in the term for new ventures—that probably at the beginning of the new term, someone would take her up on it, but at the end of a term everyone's planning holidays or vacation jobs or extra study—they don't want the sudden upheaval of new lodgings.

"She said then that she couldn't wait so long."

"*Couldn't?*" Shields stressed the word.

She nodded vehemently. "Exactly that. You can see why I jumped to the idea there definitely was a man. If she had someone who wanted her away from home so he could share the flat set-up whenever he liked, with no strings, he wasn't going to wait around for weeks and weeks.

"I asked, what was the hurry, and why did she want to leave home in the first place. I told her I thought she was wrong to go, because her home's good—I've been there—and though she has the housekeeping to do she'd still have plenty of that in a flat of her own.

"That was when she got mysterious. She said at first, 'It's because of a man.' Then she added, 'No one you know.' Then—I suppose my eyes were popping with curiosity and she realised she couldn't leave it at that, and had to fob me off with something, or I'd give her no peace—'I met him at a demonstration. A stranger. We met out there,' she gestured towards the city, 'right out of the blue, I and a stranger.' She seemed to be talking almost to herself at that point, and that was when she was half laughing, half crying, as ... as though dwelling on memories perhaps. She went on, 'He and I met and nothing's ever going to be the same again—for either of us.'

She shrugged, "What would you have made of it yourself?"

"Possibly the same as you did," he admitted, then pressed, "What else?"

She frowned. "Nothing. I was curious. I wanted his name, what he looked like—whether he was married. All she'd say was, 'I don't want to talk about it. He's no one you know. I don't want you to meet him.'

"That was as good as a slap in the eye." The dimple half showed again. "Naturally I moved off the subject fast, and I never found out anything more."

Ann Aveyard had crossed to the desk. She asked brusquely, looking down at him, "Why did you really want to know all that? You said it was curiosity, right after telling us we've wasted your time and your energy and a whole heap more of things. Why waste more time with that?" she challenged.

"Yes, why?" the challenge was taken up by Nigel Detrick. Shields dampened the rising hope in their faces with a curt, "Nothing but curiosity."

"All right," the young man's voice was rough and uneven, "all right, and I'm curious too. Tell me this, if you deal in puzzles—tell me the answer to this one, Mr. Jefferson Shields. Who armed the kids that day? That's something I want to know. How badly I want to know you can guess for yourself!"

When the older man didn't answer he banged one bunched fist on the desk. Idly Shields saw the black ballpoint pen dance across the white paper with the force of it, as Nigel Detrick's voice railed at him in bitterness, "Tell me the answer to that! I'll pay you! Someway I'll raise the money! We all will. All of us who were for non-violence that day and are saddled with this god-damn mess. All of us. We'll scrape up the money some way." He thrust the big scarred hands under the other man's nose. "I can earn money. I've told you so. I can clear land and heave bricks and cart logs till I've paid you."

The anger went. He straightened. He said huskily, "Find out—if you can," then sharply he questioned, "You've mentioned this Thought Club and I've told you what I know, but—do the police reckon it was someone from there who armed the kids? Joined the march along the route and landed us in this trouble? Tell—"

"No. They don't know how it happened."

"All right." Nigel was staring down at his hands as though judging their capabilities, their ability to pay for what he was asking, "You go there, Mr. Shields, and find out. I'll pay you. That's a promise."

CHAPTER SEVEN

The big studio was a surprise. After the long climb up the narrow, rickety, uncared for stairs with their peeling linoleum, past walls whose ochre-yellow had faded to dinginess long ago, and was now decorated with scrawled obscenities, with the smell of damp and disinterest and crowded humanity—the big square room at the top of the building, with the glass skylight letting full sunlight wash over the polished floorboards, Shields found himself simply standing inside the doorway, caught still by astonishment.

Along one wall was a bank of white painted filing cabinets. There were easy chairs, deep glowing ruby and muted green; there was one whole wall of paintings and line drawings, that ranged from the wild abstract to a delicate tracery of white and black trees above a lakeside, and there was Michael Morrow, in a neat dark business suit, the sunlight polishing the bald dome of head, blue eyes crinkled in a smile and small hand outstretched in welcome.

From the shortness of his bare five feet he looked up at Shields' tall figure, and his high voice chattered, "I had the message all right. That's what I pay the answering service for. The first time you let me down, I told them, is the last time I use you, and they know I mean it. I've heard of you of course. You want to know what I felt when I got that message that Jefferson Shields had been phoning me and that he'd call at five o'clock and hoped to find me in?" The small hands that constantly gestured as he was speaking were thrust into the air and the round face puckered into open laughter. "I got the heebies! Here, I said to myself, what've you been up to, Michael Morrow, that you could be part of a puzzle, a problem, because that's what that fellow plays with all day. Well, the answer

75

stared me in the face, of course. One of my photos has turned up on your desk, part of a puzzle, part of a problem."

Without preamble Shields said, "The photograph of Robyn Calder."

"A-ah," the sound was long-drawn, regretful. The round face grimaced. "Funnily enough," he confessed, "I didn't even consider that one. Where's the problem? The puzzle? Where's *your* interest in that?"

"I've been asked to find out who armed her."

"Anyone. Anyone with an axe to grind. Anyone who wants to make trouble—bring the police into disrepute— the old tag, you know, of police brutality, and what're they expected to do when they're faced with a riot? Pussy-foot in and say, 'Excuse me, sir and madam, but will you kindly desist from such riotous conduct?'" The room was filled with laughter, then abruptly the little man was sober again, sober and scowling. "There's that, and anyone who wants to cover up something else. A riot makes a big, big stink. It hits the headlines. You and me and Tom Brown and Uncle Joe're so busy lapping it up and licking our chops and telling one another that in our day it was different, that we all tend to overlook other bits of news— and they're usually more important than the riots."

Shields looked up alertly. He was remembering what Virtue had claimed, that during nearly every wild demonstration there had been a wild-cat strike somewhere else that had lost the country and business life uncounted contracts and good will.

The other man's answer disconcerted him. He said shrilly, "Fires." He gave a jerk of laughter. He derided, "Never given thought to it, have you? It was just idleness that started me thinking of it, actually. I was laid up. Influenza. I was bored to hell, and I was sorting through some of the old files over there," he waved towards the white bank of filing cabinets, "I've got them cross-classified, day and time as well as subject matter.

"It dawned on me, right out of the blue, how often it seemed to happen that a demonstration took place just when a fire broke out somewhere else. You might say, what about it? Fires break out every day of the week in a big city. You'd be right, of course, but you look at some that happened during these demonstrations—and remember one thing. Unless someone's killed a fire's old hat stuff. Not really interesting. Not a subject that will make people indignant and make them spend their five cents on buying your paper, because you and me and Tom Brown and Uncle Joe and the rest of us never think how much the fire cost—or if we do we say comfortably to ourselves, 'Oh well it's insured, so who's to worry.'"

The small hands had become still, linked in front of Morrow as he went on, gaze fastened on space, "If I were the police I'd change my tactics. Next time there's a demonstration, leave them to it. Block off the streets to everyone else and just leave 'em to it. Let them sit all they like and make all the speeches they like and all the hoohey they like. It's a fact, you know, that it's usually an outsider who starts things off—someone gets mad to find his way blocked and heaves and jostles, or throws a punch, or someone objects to the wording of a placard and tries to rip it up.

"Well, I wouldn't let them. Barricade the streets and let the demonstrators sit for ever. I'd have the police in the factories instead, sniffing for smoke. It might be interesting. And I wouldn't let it happen that main streets are blocked right off, so there are traffic jams everywhere else and the fire engines can't get readily through to a fire.

"Mind you," he warned, "I'm not saying there's anything in it, but it's a fact that half a dozen of the biggest and most damaging fires the city's ever had have taken place while a demonstration's been blocking the city. You and me and Tom Brown and Uncle Joe aren't interested in boots and shoes, or carpets, or panties, or pots and pans, except when we're using them. It doesn't really matter that a factory making them's gone up in smoke, because there's plenty more stocks of everything in the shops. If you ever do stop to think about the results of it, you think so many poor bastards are out of work and the business has shut down, but you don't get het-up about it, because there's always the comfortable thought that every mug's insured these days. You never stop to think that while the business is shut down they're losing orders and contracts worth a whole heap, and it's a funny thing, but most of these places are ones who're in the overseas markets. In fact, what it boils down to, there's a fire, and there's a lot of overseas contracts gone up in smoke too, and a lot of overseas money that ought to be coming into the country to keep you and me and Tom Brown and Uncle Joe prosperous."

Shields was feeling extremely tired, a tiredness, he knew, that had its roots in a grey pall of depression closing down on thought. He said, and his mouth felt stiff, as though trying to hold the words back against his will, "The same thing, in fact, as a wild-cat strike that shuts a place down."

"You've got it, and there are strikes going on, too—and every bit of it's covered up by the publicity these demonstrations are getting. Like I said before, leave the demonstrators to it. And starve them of publicity. Warn the factories, bring the police back to their real jobs, alert the decent union men to what's going on, and give the publicity, every inch of it, right down to how much the country's lost by it, to every fire, every strike, every shutdown that's happening and . . ."

He stopped. His voice had risen to a near shout. Now it was dropped again and muted as he said, and there was embarrassment in his face, "I've been riding a hobby-horse."

Unbidden, the quotation sprang to Shields' thoughts—Death, a pale horse—and he was mentally watching factories, and businesses and the country's prosperity die, and along with it he was seeing Robyn Calder—dead, too.

He said sharply, "You were there, at that demonstration, in the thick of it. How many of them were armed?"

The blue eyes blinked rapidly as though it was taking Morrow several minutes to re-orient himself, to scramble his thoughts away from what he had been speaking about.

He said at last, "Two or three—to my certain knowledge, two anyway."

"Have you told the police that?"

Morrow hesitated again. At last he admitted, "No." Then he said sharply, "Look, that sounds ridiculous perhaps, but put it alongside my hobby-horse and see how it seemed to me. If I admit this fact—publicly—what have I done? Centred more publicity on that demonstration and the students taking part in it, when I'm wondering, privately, if the whole thing wasn't engineered by someone in the background as a cover-up to something far more important.

"So I kept my mouth shut. That photo..." He grimaced. "It was instinctive to take it. I saw her holding that ... iron bar or something ... I'm not sure exactly what it was, only that she was armed. I had the camera. I snapped her. Even then I was thinking that here was an argument for my hobby-horse—that here was proof some of these kids were armed, and who armed them, and why? Who's at the back of that? You understand me, the way I was thinking?"

At the other man's brief nod he went on reflectively, "So I got out of the mess and came back here and developed the prints. I'm not contracted to any paper at all. I'm strictly freelance, so I brought the camera back here and developed that print. It was drying on the racks when I heard over the news session that a girl had died.

"Well, that was going to get publicity however you looked at it, and I thought, maybe somebody's going to collar the blame—some other kid they rounded up still armed with something. I didn't know if the girl in my snap was the same one who'd died—I waited till the evening paper came out and there was a snap of her in some party frock, in the press. I knew then she was the one I'd snapped, so I took the photo to the police. I wanted them to know that maybe she'd brought it on herself—that she'd lashed out with that thing she held and had it wrenched off her and was given a crack with it over her own silly head."

"But you didn't mention those others who were armed?" Shields reminded.

"Why should I? In that mêlée faces were just a blur. I couldn't have put a face to the blurs. To put it bluntly, I didn't want further involvement either. I handed over the photo and they questioned me—who was near the girl, did

I see her later on, did I see anyone attacking her?—I could give a no to the whole lot."

"Were the others who were armed, all students?"

"Dressed like it. Who could tell for a certainty?"

"No," Shields agreed heavily, "no one could."

He asked, "You took other photos? The police have a couple. I've seen them. They show backs—struggling figures, a few policemen..."

"That's right. I was really concentrating on the police brutality angle. I was in the road, snapping the police throwing the kids off there—and I don't mean brutally. My angle was going to be—no more force than was necessary was used, according to my camera.

"I took one of the two good snaps I got, there. They appeared in the press the following morning. You'll have seen them. I gave copies to the police."

"Yes," Shields agreed, "and there were a couple showing the march on the move. It looks orderly, as the students claim."

"Oh yes, it was that all right. Simply a line of youths and girls along the outside of the pavement."

"Did you follow it along the whole route? How did you learn there was a demonstration, in the first place?"

"To the last—" Morrow answered promptly, "one of the kids rang the press. They want publicity of course—lots of it. He told them what it was to be about, and that it was to be a peaceful demonstration etc. etc. They tipped me off."

"Were other press men there?"

"No. That's why I had the tip-off. I'm freelance. The press aren't responsible for compensation for my injuries and possible maiming." He laughed again. "They are for their own men and frankly, the press men are sick of the demonstrations anyway. You appear with a camera and everyone hates you, on the lines of 'Take a snap of me mixed up in this would you, you bastard!' and they try bashing your face in.

"It's easier to let a freelance man go along and do the dirty work. That's logic. Mind you, I had no intention of

80

getting caught up in that mob. I was meanin' to stay on the outskirts, on the road, and it was actually the police who shoved me into it. When the women started screaming, the line of police surged forward from the road. I was inside the line. I was just swept along and I finished by the fountain. Otherwise I'd not have seen the girl at all in all probability."

"Someone chased you after you'd taken the snap?" There was a dry amusement in Shields' voice.

The other man grimaced. "That's right. Just as I told you before—on the lines of 'Take a snap of me, will you, you bastard!' I got free of him though, and then funnily enough, nearly crashed into him when I did get right through the crowd.

"Look at it in terms of a whirlpool. The ones I snapped and me were whirled round in it and shot out all to one side of the crowd. I didn't realise that—I only noticed the PMG chap who'd gone after me, till I'd got the photo developed, then I recognised the middle-aged woman who'd been shot out with me, too."

Shields asked sharply, "Who else was tossed out at the same time?"

The bald head was shaken. Twice. "No one who was armed. No students, either. They were just ordinary folk, who'd wanted nothing but keeping out of it. A chap who looked like a bank-messenger-on-the-job, some women who'd been shopping, I expect, a couple of girls who'd maybe nicked out from offices to see the fun, and a few businessmen. They all scuttled off, once they had their breath back, especially when they saw my camera."

"Just ordinary people. No students. Police?"

"They were everywhere. I didn't see any by the fountain though. When I was shot out there was one big fellow standing on the pavement holding a bloody nose and cursing away to himself."

"Did you see what started the row in the first place?"

"No. I'd just taken a photo, then..." his hands were thrown up, "the world erupted."

"Return to thinking of the start of the march," Shields

urged him. "Try to picture the scene clearly. Can you see other people joining in along the route? Pressing in beside a marcher here and there, so that possibly something could have been passed to the marcher?"

"No. Quite definitely, no." Morrow kept on shaking his bald head long after he had fallen silent and long after he had lit a cigarette and taken the first long drags on it. Then he said, "If you think I can help you pinpoint who armed them, and where, you're wasting your time. I can't. I doubt if anyone could, or would be willing to. Are any of those kids going to admit ... *now* ... with Robyn Calder dead ... that anyone at all was armed? Of course they're not," he scorned the idea.

"I'll tell you one thing, though, something you might have overlooked. There's a certain type of person who's confronted with a group of marchers and who immediately gets their dander up, and says to themselves, 'Who the blazes do they think they are, hogging the way like that? Well, I'll just show them they're not owning the footway or the city or the country either while I'm here to stop them,' and quite deliberately, though they could skirt round the march easy enough, they cross the road and shove their way through the marchers to reach their destination. It's just sheer pig-headedness. They're not above thrusting out their elbows and giving a good jab in passing, either. It gives them quite a bit of satisfaction, yet to look at they're ordinary, decent blokes—and, mind you, I'm not omitting women, either. There are plenty of ordinary, decent house-wives who're like that, too—watch them some time and see them using a shopping basket or umbrella to bash their way through.

"If you think of that you can get another picture on the scene—the sort of ordinary-looking people bashing through the marchers, breaking the line for a minute, and maybe reaching in those same shopping baskets or inside a coat, fishing out something and passing it so swiftly it's not noticeable."

He fell silent again, his blue gaze bright, expectant, as it searched the other man's sallow features.

Shields asked gently, "Tell me why they should."

"You tell me, instead, because I don't know, except perhaps we're back to my hobby-horse. You think that?"

"I don't know, either, but I consider you should talk to the police—to Inspector Virtue at least. Discuss that same hobby-horse with him—no wait till I've finished. Virtue is already seriously concerned about the coincidence of strikes while the demonstration's on. He said nothing about fires. You could suggest he consider that point also. I should imagine there's been top level talks about the strikes, at the very least, already. Tell me, why haven't you already given the police a hint of what you have been thinking?"

The other man jumped up and began to move round the room in short, jerky strides. His hands were gesticulating again as he spoke, admitting, "Because I've been afraid of being called a fool. Perhaps, to be brutally honest, because I fancied, too, that maybe I could outsmart them—go to them in the end and throw a whole lot of proof into their faces about my hobby-horse and ask them why they've been sitting on their bums when all this's been going on under their noses."

There was silence. Through the open skylight sound came to them, of the busy city outside. Shields let his gaze travel round the room in slow appraisal, and abruptly the other man asked, "Surprised this room should be up here on top of all that down below?" his thumb jerked downwards.

"Yes," Shields admitted mildly, his gaze lifting in question.

"It's cheap. It's central, too. I could go somewhere else and pay four times the price and have four times less privacy. No one bothers me here. A dago owns it. He gets his countrymen off the migrant boats and shoves them here, a whole family to a room at a time. Both sides are happy about it. The owner gets a living, the families get a roof till they find something better. All they're intent on is doing that, and getting a job for papa and the bigger boys in the family. Then they go. They never bother me. It suits me." He grinned. "I can get drunk, play the radio all night, have a woman here, all night, too—nobody's interested."

Abruptly he demanded, "What's really in all this for you? Where's the problem? Where's the puzzle? Who's your client? What are you going to do next—where are you going from here?" He had obviously hoped to catch the other man off guard, but Shields merely smiled.

He said, "I want to know who armed Robyn Calder—and the others you saw. The students themselves have asked me." He saw something that looked like disappointment in the blue eyes and questioned sharply, "What reason did you think I have?"

The other shrugged. "I was guessing. I thought perhaps it would be Calder—the girl's father—wanting to fix blame somewhere." In an attempt at explanation he added, "He's a bit by the way of the hellfire and brimstone inclination I'd say—the Lord will bring justice down on the sinner type of attitude. The sinner will be revealed and the sin revealed in the light of the day, etc. etc."

The faint mockery in his voice died away. He said soberly, "No, that's unjust—giving you the wrong impression. He doesn't go round bible-thumping so far as I know. It was just ... I went to see him, you know. No, you wouldn't know," he brushed that aside, "but I did. I wanted to hear what the girl had told him about these demonstrations. She was armed, you see. I wanted to know if he knew anything about that; how it had happened; if she'd ever talked to him about other demonstrations. It was my hobby-horse riding me again, you understand, but I should have guessed he'd know nothing.

"I talked to him. I put my foot in it. The police hadn't told him about that photo. I don't know why. Perhaps they'd been hoping it needn't come out, that he could be spared knowing about it. Anyway they hadn't told him—then, at any rate. When I mentioned the photo he said, quite calmly, 'You're telling a lie.'

"He imagined I was some reporter trying to make a further sensation out of the girl's death. I had to show him a print of the photo before he'd believe it, and all he said was that obviously she'd found the bar on the ground some-where, where someone else had dropped it, and she was scared for her safety in the crowd, and had picked it up, as protection.

"That's so much nonsense. Oh, not about her being scared, but you couldn't have bent to pick up something in that mêlée—you'd have been knocked flat and trampled under-foot. I tried to make him see that, but he wouldn't.

"He's stubborn, and righteous. He insisted that evil always rebounds on the evil-doer, and that those who had taken arms into the crowd would be suitably punished. It wasn't thrown at me in a ranting way—just as a statement of assured fact. I thought he might have decided to help justice along a bit, and had asked you to find who'd done the arming, and who'd been armed."

"No. I haven't seen him. What do you know about a place called the Thought Club?"

The blue eyes narrowed. For a moment there was only silence, then Morrow said slowly, "Not much. So they're involved somewhere, are they?"

"I don't claim so." The rebuke was sharp, but the other man only grinned.

"You don't claim your mum and dad were white folks. That's obvious," was the tart rejoinder. "Come off it. Oh, all right, you can have what I know. That's about nothing. Two men run it. Rex Bratton's a Commie. All for the brotherhood of man, the equal distribution of the world's goods and solemnity for all. Have you ever noticed these avowed Commies never seem to know how to laugh? You get the idea that if you told them a ribald yarn about the boss taking his secretary to Surfer's for the weekend, they'd only ask what expense was incurred, and how much of a share of it rightly belonged to the workers.

"Well, as I stated, he's a Commie. He's so blatant about it you merely say Poohey and dismiss him, and yet ... I'm always suspicious of anyone who's too obviously a type. Brat-ton's exactly that. The other is Athol Lesie. At a glance you'd put him neatly into another type-class—good prep school, private and expensive high school, a good ground-

85

ing in subjects dealing with commerce, and a comfortable and ordinary private life.

"The club's as obviously a type as they are. It's a coffee shop—open to anyone and a restaurant of the type that opens about midday and goes on to midnight. The place is clean, the food good—and the price varies according to the hour. There's no liquor licence. You bring your own, if you're so inclined. Entertainment is strictly an evening concern—folk singers, anyone with talent—I mean that—they don't have anyone obviously untalented.

"Artists are encouraged to line the walls with their work. No charge, except if one gets sold they take a cut for the club.

"At a glance it's a meeting and discussion place for the arts and the intellectuals. You can talk there without being drowned out by catwauling and noisy bands.

"There's no gambling. There's never been a whisper of suspicion about drug-passing, or a brawl, or it being a place where you'd see obvious crooks or where a lot of the women are professionals." He grinned. "Unaccompanied women are strictly barred—that's a fact. Now tell me what you think that all comes down to."

Shields shook his head. He suggested, "Are you prejudiced against them because they organise these demonstrations? They seem very innocent."

The other man shrugged, "I'm not prejudiced. I just don't know anything much about them—except what I've told you—which is what anyone knows. There's nothing against them, or their organising. They talk peace. No arming."

Shields stood up. He said regretfully, "I've taken a great deal of your time—to no purpose."

"Yours, too," the other shot back. "You know, if it was me, I'd drop it. You'll never get anyone to admit anything about that day, not now, not when the girl's dead."

"Perhaps not. Tell me, what other demonstrations have you attended? Have you filed photos of those events, also?" His gaze was on the white bank of files.

For a brief minute Morrow hesitated, then he said, "Yes.

I've been to others, I've photos and some of them are of people armed. No, I didn't take them to the police. I've told you why not. It'd only give more publicity. You want to see them?" He warned, "There aren't any of the girl."

"What about people you've seen at the Thought Club?"

Morrow asked impatiently, "Who have I seen there who wouldn't look different in a demonstration march? When you're dining out you don't wear the same clothes, or the same face, come to that, as when you're marching." Almost angrily, he demanded, "Do you want prints of these?" He was holding a single manilla folder he had taken from one filing case. "They're all in here—all the armed ones. Some are just backs. No two show the same person and there's no one I recognise."

"The students at the University might. Yes, I want prints."

"All right, I'll do them tonight. I'll send them to you in the morning. Is that good enough?"

He was still standing in the open doorway, still holding the manilla folder, when Shields looked back from the curve of the rickety staircase. The words floated down to the older man in mockery, "You don't give me much credit for using my head, do you? Of course I've asked round for clues from the students myself."

The door slammed shut, cutting off light to the stairwell, so that Shields had to go down gropingly, one hand against the scrawled and peeling walls.

CHAPTER EIGHT

The Calder house was small and neat—white painted brick, set well back from the low brick wall, the face of the house sheltered from prying eyes by two big trees pressing close to the front windows.

There was a man working in the front garden when Jefferson Shields first approached the place. He stopped, appraising the house, and the man, listening to the shrill whine of the power mower being driven in wide sweeps up and down the front lawn.

The sun was dying. It lay blood-red and brazen, deep on the skyline to one side of the house. The flaring rays of it burned the walking figure to sun-bronzed skin, and a bulk that he did not actually possess. Only when Shields opened the gate and walked towards the other man did he see that the skin was actually pale, with a scatter of fine dark hairs on the bare arms below the rolled-up shirt-sleeves. There was thick dark hair showing in the open neck of the shirt, below the square chin, but the man's head was almost as bare as Michael Morrow's—with only a fringe of receding darkness at the back.

Because of the mower he hadn't heard the gate. When he became aware of the visitor he literally jumped, the blue eyes widening in startled surprise.

A jerk of his hand silenced the mower. He stood staring, motionless, silent and waiting.

Jefferson Shields gave his name and elicted no response except a murmured, "Good evening."

Shields asked, "Alexander Calder?" and the balding head jerked acknowledgment, while the gaze turned wistfully back to the mower and then to the lengthening shadows across the grass and the dying sun in the west. He said heavily at last, "You wanted to see me? What about then?"

"Your daughter," Shields told him bluntly and the other's body jerked again.

The features went completely blank. He said, as though the formula was something he'd grown accustomed to use, "I have nothing to say whatsoever and I do not wish to discuss the matter." His hand began to slide towards the mower again.

Shields told him, "I've been asked by Nigel Detrick, a friend and co-student of your daughter's, and by Christine Stowe, another such—to find out why your daughter died."

The hand stopped quite still. Abruptly the other man turned on his heel. He said curtly, "You'd better come in," but he barely waited till they had gone through the screen door and into the narrow hall before he demanded, "What do you mean, about *why* she died!" He turned, still in the hall, to face the other frowningly, "The point's obvious, isn't it? She attended a demonstration. That's why she died."

"No. She died because some of the students were armed. As your daughter was. That was totally unexpected—a factor that should never have entered the demonstration at all. Detrick and Miss Stowe—other students, also—who were involved, want to know how it happened, and why."

Alexander Calder thought that over in slow appraisal, the fingers of his left hand pulling at his lower lip. Then he said, "Yes, I see. You've a point there. It's something I've thought about, you know, but there didn't seem ... well, what could anyone do? I've met Detrick. That girl—Christine Stowe, too. No, not—not since it happened. Not since Robyn died. I just couldn't bring myself to face any of them, except a few I invited to the service. I thought if I didn't do that it would seem I hated the lot of them and ... well, it's bitterness, you see. I can't stop myself blaming them and hoping they'll be punished. I've wanted to see them punished. I've been waiting for someone to do something. There's the inquest next week," he went on rapidly, "and I've been hoping that the blame would be brought home then fair and square, and that the guilty ones—the ones who started the riot and armed the others—will be caught out." He sounded angry when he said, "And now you come saying *they've* asked you to find things." He spoke as though his anger was for having his waiting disturbed, his ideas upset, his hope of vengeance and punishment brought to nothing.

Again he said, turning towards a door on the right, "You'd better come in."

The room was small, well furnished with modern teak furniture. The plum-coloured carpet looked new; so did the cushions that were arranged with stiff care on the low settee.

Calder hesitated. He asked, "You'd like a drink? I usually stick to beer, before dinner..." His glance was questioning. When Shields nodded, he went out of the room. He was gone only a moment, to return with two frosted cans, and two glasses, on a small metal tray.

Pouring, handing one glass to Shields, he demanded sharply, "If those students don't *know* who brought arms into the march, have they any *idea* who did?"

"No," Shields admitted, and probed, "Have you?"

The startled pale eyes turned to meet his. "Me? Of course not. How could I?"

"Didn't Robyn talk to you of these demonstrations?"

Calder sat down in one of the low chairs, leaning back, his gaze now on the drink in his hand. "Yes. She was growing up. Beginning to think for herself. Our ideas often clashed. She'd think one way, I'd think another. I suppose that's the usual thing. I had to pull myself up sometimes; remind myself she wasn't just a kid any more." He lifted his gaze. He said simply, "We were happy together."

After a moment he went on, "There was never any talk of violence, except generally. I'd say it was pretty crook about what happened in some march in particular, and ask if she could guess how it had come about. Robyn, of course, defended the demonstrators. I could see her point. It's a fact, you know, it's often some outsider who picks a fight because he thinks ... well, he has his own ideas, you see, and he

90

thinks because he's older he can give a kid—a student—a good kick in the pants for thinking different." He frowned down at the glass. "I've seen a couple, from the outskirts. People are funny, you know, the way they..." he seemed set to ramble on in low-voiced reflection, but Shields cut him short, asking:

"Didn't you object? You must have realised that one day she might be hurt, surely?"

"Of course I objected!" Then he shook his head. "But look, you can only run rein on someone else to just so far. Robyn's conscience told her these demonstrations were worthwhile and she could put up a good argument and like I said, I had to remember she wasn't a kid any more. I didn't like the way she went about expressing her arguments in public. I said so, forcibly sometimes and yet ... if she thought it worthwhile to face possible injury for these causes, doesn't it show she thought pretty deeply about the issues involved?

"Look at it this way." He stopped. He began again in a harder voice, "I've had a lot of anonymous letters and phone calls, you know. They've said I'm to blame for her death, because I didn't stop her going and why didn't I control my own daughter. I refuse to accept that's right. The way I thought of it was—were you in the war?" he demanded.

"Yes."

"So was I. In the thick of it. We risked injury all the time and death, too—didn't we?" A faint smile touched his mouth. "I don't suppose any of us took time to work out motives and so on, but we must have thought the game was worth it, or we'd have cut out and done a blue, wouldn't we, to get away from the hell of it? Well, the war's over. Our war, that is. But this new lot of kids faces others, and a lot of other things, too. If they find something worth fighting for .... well..." He shrugged. "That's how I argued. I just warned her that if she did get hurt she'd have to blame herself."

"Didn't she ever try to find out how the demonstrations got out of hand?" Shields pressed.

"Yes, but what could she do. There was no point where she could start. She thought, as I did, it was maybe a case of hooligans—the type who honestly enjoy bashing and hurting and destroying just for the hell of it."

Dryly Shields asked, "Didn't she ever reflect that if the demonstrations stopped the riots would, also?"

"I put that point to her. Robyn didn't agree. She stated—she had a good argument there—that if they didn't have the demonstrations to shield them those hooligan types'd still destroy and fight among themselves. That's true enough. Remember the gang fights between youths of only a few years back? That seems to have died down recently. Her idea was that at least the point of the demonstrations—the reason for them—was brought home pretty forcibly to the public."

Suddenly impatient, he thrust the empty glass aside and demanded, "What does all that matter now? You want to know how everyone got armed, that last time and I can't help you."

Shields placed his own glass neatly beside the other on the metal tray. He asked abruptly, "Was she leaving home because there was a man in her life—someone you disliked?"

The surprise seemed genuine. Calder jerked. "Where'd you get that idea? It's nonsense. What's the point of the question?" he demanded.

"Just that my enquiries into all this led me to discussing your daughter with everyone concerned. I learned that she was leaving home, that she spoke of a man who had entered her life and had changed it completely."

This time he was quite sure that the astonishment was genuine. Calder simply stared blankly, then he shook his head. He said slowly at last, "It's nonsense. I've never heard of him. There's never been a mention of him. Never a sign of him. If there'd been someone he'd have come to see me when she died."

He seemed incapable of thinking that there could be reasons why that hadn't happened. He simply said in the same puzzled voice, "I don't know how that story grew up around her, but it's not true. Anyway it doesn't help you, does it?"

Shields didn't answer. Instead he demanded, "What do you know of the Thought Club? Did Robyn go there frequently?"

"The Thought Club?" Again he seemed puzzled. He said, "I've never heard of it. What is it?"

"A meeting place for people interested in the arts, intellectual matters, demonstrations..."

"I've never heard of it," Calder objected again.

"It's quite well known to the University people—the students. I'm told the food is good, the entertainment, also —that it's a recognised place for good dining, for..."

Calder dismissed that with a curt, "Robyn didn't go out much of an evening. She liked being at home." He seemed to be remembering aloud as he went on, "We played chess. Robyn was very good at it, and we talked and sometimes some of the neighbours'd drop in after dinner and we'd have a go at the cards, though she wasn't so fond of that, and she'd leave us and go to the kitchen and come on back later with something new she'd made for our supper. She was always collecting recipes out of the magazines and books." He blinked. He said heavily, "But you don't want to hear about that sort of thing."

He said, as he had done in the beginning, "I've been waiting for the blame to be put somewhere, and the punishment dealt out to them. Don't you think," he asked suddenly, "that Detrick has handed you a red herring? Don't you reckon that perhaps he's just trying to run from trouble— that he's out to show that he and the others are lily white and innocent of anything to do with that arming?"

He sounded angry now. The pale gaze challenged the other man with a defiant, "How do you know it isn't that and that you're wasting time, and that he's laughing at you right now for being fool enough to fall for the pap he's handed out to you?"

He stood up, so sharply that the chair rocked. He said flatly, "If you ask me, Detrick knows quite well who armed them that day. He's thrown a fish to you and you've swallowed it ... whole." His expression expressed nothing but a bitter contempt.

When there was no answer he demanded, "Now you've thought that over, don't you agree with me?"

"No," Shields objected mildly. He added, standing up, collecting his neat grey felt hat from the table, "No, because I keep reflecting on the fact that at these demonstrations there are few *oral* reports of arming. I stress that, because invariably, it seems, there are pictorial records of such arming. Don't you consider it an amazing coincidence, Mr. Calder, that the very people who are armed are the ones who are photographed? Out of all those milling crowds?"

.   .   .

John Virtue's voice, over the phone, was bitter.

He admitted, "We've noticed it. We noticed it a long time ago. The fire brigade sends in full reports of course. We're only too aware that it's the ones with overseas contracts that go up in smoke—just at the worst possible time for those same contracts."

He said, "Yes, you're quite right in thinking we've had top level talks. That's been our main point—rather than the strikes. I didn't want to admit it to you." There was faint apology in the confession, "I told you enough, so I thought, to whet your interest in that damn Thought Club. I wish Morrow hadn't caught on to it. It's obvious people are starting wondering, in some circles..."

"What have you done about it?" Shields pressed.

"All we can. We've warned, so far as we're able, without blaring the thing from the housetops, so that everyone up top is alerted and the thing is stopped before we nail someone.

"It's an impossible situation. The fires always break out where the brigades have a terrific job getting to them, because of the clogged traffic. When they do arrive there's another crowd out of hand, milling around, staring—and no police, because they're all elsewhere dealing with the demonstration riot.

"In the main it's a matter for internal security in the

factories themselves, you know. We can do just so much, but how can you have every factory in the country with police in every nook and cranny of the place, watching for trouble? It's impossible and we all know it. It's up to the factory people themselves—to clamp down on possible trouble-makers and put them where they're under supervision, and to try and control the movements of everyone in the place, but you must know yourself the real men behind this sort of thing are never obvious. They're apparently decent, law-abiding, hard workers—oh, all the rest of the honest flapdoodle that's just a cover.

"All we know is, a fire breaks out. The brigades are hampered reaching the scene, and hampered setting up their hoses even, because of the crowds—and how much of that business is stage-managed, too? Then they sometimes manage to get the fire under control—just as it breaks out somewhere else, and then a third place goes up. We can't even prove it's arson.

"It's an impossible set-up to police, even if we had the men. Once the first fire breaks out it's a case of everyone out at the double. How could we go in to search the place for possible delayed fuses, or remote control devices?

"Myself, I'd plump for manual control anyway. That's where I'm hoping we'll strike lucky and get someone. You see, you can't gauge wind, or know it will stay in one direction; you can't know how far the first fire'll go, or what'll collapse—remote control or delayed fuses might be destroyed, and break out in an area already firing, while another section's safe, due to a wind change. It's too chancy. You could finish up with main buildings hardly hurt."

He added, "I'll pull Morrow in and make him shut up. Another thing, I'd like to see what photos he's taken at fires, though if he's been attending the demonstrations he couldn't be at both points at once—he must turn up at the fires when they're nearly over. We've already collated all the fire photos we can from television and press sources. They're not helpful." He demanded, "Are you going to visit Lesie and Bratton?"

"Yes." Almost apologetically, Shields added, "Nigel Detrick has become my client. He asked me to go there. He wants me to tell him who armed the students—Robyn Calder, in particular."

There was a jerk of laughter. Virtue said lightly, "So I don't have to urge? But don't be too impressed by Detrick's professed blue-eyed innocence. Just remember that the inquest's coming forward next week and unless he manages to throw suspicion from himself he's likely to find himself outside the University. Once that photo of the girl is released there'll be a howl to heaven that won't die down until the University cracks down somewhere. What's the betting, just between us, that the crack lands on Detrick, and that he knows the answer to the question of the arming already?"

Almost primly Shields told him, "I never bet."

There was another soft chuckle. "You'll get along fine with Rex Bratton then. According to him betting is a capitalistic dodge to relieve the working man of the fruits of his honest toil and detour it into the pockets of the wicked Government and big business and keep the worker enslaved in poverty. Possibly I have the jargon a little mixed, but no doubt you'll get the message.

"Shields," now his voice was quite sober, the mockery gone, "watch your step. That place is a front for something, and no one goes to the trouble of building up a front and keeping it going, if the something behind it is honest. Goodbye, good luck, too."

CHAPTER NINE

Christine Stowe said, "I intend to marry Nigel, you know." She gave a little grimace when her companion merely gave a lift of one grey eyebrow, then she laughed, and the dimple came back to her cheek. She said lightly, "I honestly thought I'd make you jump with surprise with that statement. I wanted to. Your ... unflappability ... is that the word I want? Well, it's rather ... challenging, you know."

Jefferson Shields smiled at her quite kindly. He had chosen to have the girl accompany him that evening, rather than either Ann or Nigel, but his gaze had already picked out the other couple at a table the far side the room. He had guessed that Nigel's curiosity, his anxiety, would prove too great for him to keep away, but from either indifference or defiance, the boy had chosen to turn up in an ancient windcheater over slacks and an open-necked shirt.

At that hour of the evening—after eight o'clock—he was one of only three men so dressed. There was a good scatter of neat business suits, a few polo-necked sweaters under plain jackets, and the rest had at least made the effort to look passably well dressed.

The girls were invariably dressed up. Ann had chosen a grey linen shift with big brass buttons; Christine an even dressier outfit of long black skirt topped with a high-necked, long sleeved, tucked and frilled blouse. She looked demure, and under the soft light of the clubroom, quite beautiful.

Looking at her with appreciation, her companion said, "I had already noticed your proprietary air towards him."

She looked startled. "Good lord, am I that obvious?"

"No. You were merely off-guard in my office. You were extremely irritated, also, by Detrick's apparent denseness on some points. How long have you known him?"

Her slim fingers were playing with the stem of her glass. She didn't look at him as she answered, "Since I came to the University."

"And Ann Aveyard?"

She said shortly, "I'm very fond of Ann. Don't make any mistake on that point. Also, don't run away with the idea that I'm trying to undermine her—take something that belongs to her. Nigel was drawn to her because he ... was sorry for her, perhaps ... protective anyway, a whole lot of things bound up with the fact she's had a rotten time, and because she's essentially a fine person she's taken it all with her chin in the air. Nigel—anyone, myself included—could admire that attitude very much. Just the same there's nothing else to bolster up the attraction. Ann's going to find her feet again and discover other friends, and Nigel will see she's all right and he'll drift away. That," she concluded with a quick smile, "is where I'll step back into the picture.

"You know, or rather you don't and maybe you'll find it hard to believe, but Nigel is strictly stodge. I don't mean that in any derogatory sense, but he's the type who is essentially law-abiding, and in a few years he's going to be a solicitor on the way up, with a neat home in the suburbs, a mortgage and a wife—me. Because I'm strictly stodge, too. Laugh if you like, but my ambition's strictly Nigel, that same mortgaged brick-veneer in a nice suburb, three kids and mothers' meetings."

His gaze was going slowly round the room. He asked, "So the University course will be wasted on you?"

"No," she denied that sharply. "If I get my B.A. I'd like to go on to pre-school kindergarten teaching. It'd fit in nicely with the sort of life I'm planning."

His attention came back to her. He asked, "What kind of a rotten time—you spoke of it as such, remember— has Ann Aveyard experienced?"

"So you don't know?" She sounded surprised. "Oliver Harrap's the cause of it. She was Oliver's girlfriend—hence she got mixed up with the University crowd, and Nigel and myself and the rest of us. She's known Oliver for years, and to see them together—well, you'd have said they were going on for years more together, quite contentedly. Then this trouble blew up. All of a sudden Oliver got his call-up papers and he tore them up and refused to go to camp and he laid claim in the courts to being a Conshie. Ann was frantic. She was dead against it, and it made things impossible for her with her family. Her father's a career soldier for one thing, and one brother's a naval officer. To put it briefly, there was hell to pay, and when Oliver was sent to prison her whole family turned on him, and Ann, too."

"Did she take part in this demonstration?" Shields asked sharply.

"No. She's tried to remain on good terms with her family, because they've always been close. If they'd found out she'd joined a demonstration advocating kicking the national service act in the teeth they'd have had a fit. Besides ... I did say, didn't I, that Ann was against Oliver's attitude?"

She shook her head, "Just the same, thinking a man is being a fool doesn't mean you fall out of love with him. Ann's still pining for him. She'll go on pining. You know, I think Oliver will just be quietly released in a little while. The government will have made its point and so will Oliver, and though it might sound crazy, I wouldn't be at all surprised if he doesn't finally go to the War zones somewhere with the Red Cross—something of that type."

"Then Ann Aveyard's family will be appeased, the lovers will come together, Nigel Detrick will be free of any entanglements, and you will take your place at his side?"

The dimple showed again. She said, in mockery at herself and the words, "And we'll all live happily ever after." Then she said sharply, "You haven't been really listening, have you? You've been gazing at something—someone—all the time..."

"Certainly I've listened." There was faint rebuke in the grey gaze turned to hers. "There is one point I wish to raise in connection with what you've said. Firstly though— yes, I have been gazing at someone. Turn your head casually. Who is the dark man to your left, near the painting of what appears to be a mechanical problem?"

The dimple showed again. After a casual slow inspection towards her left, she turned back to her companion.

"Athol Lesie," she said briefly.

"I imagined so. He has been talking to another man —short, fair, bearded. Rex Bratton?" he suggested.

"It sounds like it."

He informed her, "They know very well who I am. They have been watching this table. Have any of you mentioned that I have become involved in this?"

She looked embarrassed, then confessed, "I expect most of us know. Nigel's been rather boasting about it. He's ... frightened, you know," suddenly there was only a desperate anxiety in the girl. She said helplessly, "He's going to be ruined, you know, unless this ... this monkey is shifted off his back. Mr. Shields—"

He broke across the desperation with a quiet, "Tell me, you've been to Robyn Calder's home as a guest?"

"Yes." She was frowning, angry he knew quite well, because her plea and her anxiety had been so brutally cut short.

"What is your opinion of Mr. Calder? He spoke to me of being in the war. Most parking police are veterans, of course. Many are physically disabled. Have you ever discovered his attitude to pacifists? To Oliver Harrap for instance?"

The frown remained, but she answered readily enough, "He has no use for them. Oh, not Oliver in particular. I don't think I've been to the house since that case blew up, but I do remember discussing ... I can't think what started it, but there was a discussion one evening about the call-ups and so on and Mr. Calder became quite ... rabid, on the subject of men who shirked. I remember Robyn said something about conscience, but he wouldn't allow for that in that context at all. You either went to the wars as you were told or you were a coward and a deserter and a traitor. That was his attitude. What made you ask about it?"

"I wondered if Oliver Harrap had friends, who like him were conscientious objectors? Did Robyn Calder ever attend a pacifist demonstration? Or one demonstration against the Vietnam war? There have been several I can remember. Is it possible she met some man, a stranger, at one such demonstration, and that he was a conscientious objector—a man she would never dare take home to meet her father?"

"How odd I never thought of that!" Now the frown was gone in genuine interest. "Yes it's possible—quite possible."

"Possible, also, that if the man had gone to prison, she would want to write to him, receive letters from him, visit him—without her father knowing, so that she might realise the best solution was to leave home?"

"Yes. Yes, and yes again!" she exclaimed. The blonde hair swung at her quick nods. "That's why there's been no sign of him since she died, of course—he couldn't attend the funeral, or go to see Mr. Calder—we should have thought of it for ourselves."

"You would have, if you hadn't been trying to think of an excuse to come to me with a tale of murder by demonstration," was the tart retort.

The fair skin coloured. She didn't answer.

After a moment he asked, "She was fond of her father? Or rather ... were you aware that Mr. Calder is her uncle?"

A little grimace tightened her mouth. "Lord, yes. Very much aware. Mr. Calder told me. I ... yes, I saw a photo of Mrs. Calder. That's how we got on to the subject. He said quite casually, 'That's my late wife—Robyn's aunt,' which sounded mixed up, but he went on to explain that Robyn was his brother's girl and that he and Mrs. Calder had brought her up when her mother had run off and left her. Quite a nasty little story, and I thought it a bit hot the way he talked about it to Robyn's friends. Her mother vanished when Robyn was only nine months old. She ran off with a chap who deserted his wife and two small children for her. Oh yes, it happens every day I expect, but you don't like hearing it in connection with someone you know.

"Robyn walked into the room while he was telling me about it, and he got all sloppy then, putting his arm round her, saying what a joy she'd been to himself and Mrs. Calder, praising her for taking over the house when his wife had died suddenly. Things like that. Robyn was devoted to him. She told me often how lonely he was since Mrs. Calder died. I think that's why she stayed home so much—to keep him company. She used to say how much she owed him for bringing her up—things like that.

"Yes, you're quite right. It all fits in. She'd be terribly upset if she fell for a man who was a Conshie, and had gone to prison for it. She'd dread hurting Mr. Calder. No wonder she was up one minute and down the next, that last week—I guess it was like being torn in two parts, a tussle between her feelings for the man and for Mr. Calder. Horrid!" Her voice was soft, distressed. She said suddenly, "Life's rather beastly, isn't it?" Then, realising his attention had wandered again, she asked sharply, "What is it you're staring at?"

"Lesie is crossing this way. I think he is going to stop here. How well do you know him?"

"Only by name. By sight. By hearing others talk."

As Shields had expected, the younger man stopped by their table. The soft lighting of the room was as kind to him as it was to the girl, making the round, pale, smooth-skinned face look very young. He was wearing the same square-framed, black-rimmed glasses that Shields was beginning to think of as a badge of expressed respectability, of steadiness, of maturity, though the wearer in reality might be far different from the appearance he was trying to create.

His build was heavier and shorter than Shields had expected from seeing him across the room. There was an almost hulking bulk to his shoulders, and his neck was thick and short. He carried his head as though trying to offset the defect and his lack of more than moderate height—with the chin tilted, the dark head slightly back.

The voice was good—crisp, assured, well modulated. There was a hint of challenge in the abrupt, "You haven't been here before, have you, Mr. Shields?"

"No."

The older man didn't give him the satisfaction of asking how he had known who the visitor was, or a chance to explain his knowledge. He said, "I'd like to talk to you."

"Feel free. I'm available to anyone, any time. Would you rather come to my office? I warn you, it's not as comfortable as in here," he waved a hand round them, "but it's quieter, more private—if your talk needs that."

Shields stood up without commenting. He smiled down at the girl. "Will you wait for me?"

Lesie said gently, "I'd prefer she came with us. Other guests might not realise she wasn't alone. We have a rule about unescorted women. They can be embarrassed." His gaze challenged the other man, "And they can prove an embarrassment. I refuse to have even a whisper of trouble touch the Club."

He led the way across the room to teak louvre doors to one side, unlocked them, taking a key from a ring he was holding in his hand, and ushered them through. The corridor they faced was bleak, chill after the warmth of the clubroom, uncarpeted, barely lighted.

Lesie locked the door behind them. He said in explanation, "I don't encourage trouble. The safe's in my office." He went ahead, to a small door on the right.

As he had warned them, the small office wasn't comfortable. There was plain lino on the floor, two hard backed chairs, as well as one behind the small desk. Besides that, a telephone, and the hulking bulk of a black-fronted safe, the place was bare.

Lesie waved them to chairs—the girl to the one behind the desk. He offered cigarettes from a pack taken from his jacket pocket. When they were declined he lit one himself, crossing one leg over the other, his gaze on the other man.

"Well?" he challenged.

"How does it come about that these demonstrations almost invariably end in trouble? That there is a violence? That some, at least, of the participants, are armed?" Shields began bluntly.

The heavy shoulders lifted and fell. "You tell me, I'll

tell you." There was no mockery, only a flat statement. "I'm speaking, of course, only for the demonstrations I arrange myself, when I say there's every precaution taken against anything like that. You can take all the precautions in the world, though, and you're still faced with outsiders. You've no control over them, no knowledge of what they might do."

"How do you arrange things?"

"Quite simply. We learn what purpose the demonstration has. That for a starter. We make sure the people are genuine about it. We have complete lists of all types of organisations, clubs, societies. We contact those whose aims run on the same or similar lines.

"You could say," he assured, "that we act as agents to bring people of one aim together. Usually those we contact express a desire to join in the march and activity. Occasionally not, for one reason or another. When we know who wants to come into it, we arrange a date and time suitable for everyone.

"We can have speeches arranged, written, supplied, but usually that's not necessary. We do insist on vetting all the material used, though. If someone goes outside the stuff we've vetted, we never handle them again. We insist the speeches are to be non-inflammatory, non-defamatory. The same with any placards. We supply those if we're asked, also—we have a signwriter who does an excellent job at cut rates for us. Any placards brought into the affair by others have to be vetted by us. We reserve the right to destroy any we consider offensive, or inflammatory, or defamatory.

"We have one meeting at least—sometimes more—before the day, with all participants attending. The tactics to be followed are thrashed out—destination of the march, whether that can be dispensed with and a simple assembling arranged at some destination—the duration, the speeches, the behaviour in general.

"Arming, violence, even self-defence, is out. Quite definitely out, out *out*! Oh yes, even self-defence." His nod was quite definite. "We hammer at them with the simple truth that if you strike back when you're attacked, it's an invitation for the attacker to really wade into you. He has a bruise, a cut to show for it, hasn't he? He can claim you attacked first. He's going to have a difficult job claiming it if he's unmarked and the blows are all on the other chap.

"So you see—nothing *should* go wrong."

Shields had heard the door open behind him, and he had seen the girl's gaze turn sharply and hold behind him, too. He was prepared for the deep voice that said brusquely, "The demonstrations are deliberately sabotaged. You can't get away from that fact."

Shields didn't bother turning and after a moment the speaker rounded the chairs and came to sit on a corner of the desk.

Once in the bare office, away from the soft lighting of the clubroom, the older man had realised that Athol Lesie, for all his appearance of youth, was at least thirty. This other man looked young, too, at casual glance. It was only when one looked past the youthful glow of golden beard and hair and eyebrows, and saw the lines round the blue eyes, and the hardness there, that another ten years were added to the first summing-up of the early twenties.

Rex Bratton's build was slighter than Lesie's and his shoulders were rounded and slumped as he sat on the desk corner, the hard blue gaze challenging Shields to deny what he had just claimed.

"How?" Shields demanded bluntly.

"God knows." The retort was equally blunt.

Slyly Lesie taunted, "I thought you claimed there isn't a God, Rex—to know."

Shield thought cynically, as the gold-bearded man smiled and then laughed, that this was a common opening for this pair—the statement and parry and laughter had about it the patness, the faint tarnishing, of the parry and thrust of a pair of stage performers.

He asked, "Do you mean to state that in all these months, a year, two years—for that length of time you have never found out why and how and who does the sabotage?"

Deliberately he put doubt and open cynicism into the question.

If he had hoped for anger, he was disappointed, because both of them simply chorused, "No."

Lesie added, "We've tried. Dear lord, how we've tried!" He threw up his hands in despair. "We've arranged for monitors—people we can trust—to patrol the route of marches, to mingle on the outskirts of a crowd, but ... it still goes on. There's one spurt of anger somewhere, and if you've ever seen a demonstration yourself, with the crowd of by-standers, and police and sticky-beaks, all getting in one another's road round the demonstration, you'll know how difficult it is to keep an eye on anything at all. So a spark flares and—bam! Wham!"

"These monitors—they've seen someone armed?" Again the cynicism and doubt.

"No—not until it's too late. When a free for all starts suddenly they'll see someone armed with something, and then almost instantly whoever it is is lost in the crowd. Anyway, it's too late by then to do anything."

"Except remember what the person looked like—to pick him out from a line-up of everyone who took part—after the demonstration was over. To remember, to pick out, and to question. Well?"

"What do you take us for?" The deep-voiced question came from Bratton, in contempt. "You think we're such fools we haven't thought of anything *you* might catch on to ... now. Like you said, we've had a long time to watch things going wrong and to try and find out where and why it's happening and who's doing it. Of course we've thought of that—but faces ... you look a whole lot different when you're glaring and snarling at someone, you know. We've only ever picked out two we can really challenge, and in both cases they claimed that in the crowd someone bashed into them, cried, 'Take this!' and it was automatic to grab at what was thrust at them, and they didn't realise, till a few seconds after, that it was a weapon of some sort. By then they weren't sure who'd bashed into them, or yelled at them, or thrust the thing at them."

106

"You believed that?"

"It's quite possible, isn't it? In fact, it's a very good way of doing it, wouldn't you say?" Lesie asked.

Shields agreed. "Quite plausible, but still plausible even if not true."

Lesie shrugged. "We had no reason for doubting it."

"And then what?" When they simply gazed at him, he asked impatiently, "What happened after they realised they were now armed? Did they drop the weapons? Hold on to them? Hand them to the police? To you?"

"One said he dropped it quick-smart, then wished he hadn't, because someone else might have grabbed hold of it and used it," Bratton answered. "The other said simply and bluntly that he held on to it. He felt that if there was going to be arming all round, that he wanted something to protect his own skin. That's reasonable." With a sudden grin, he added, "I might do the same, given a riot and myself in it and the sight of a bicycle chain or a piece of lead piping."

"Do you take part in these demonstrations yourself?"

They chorused, "No." It was loud and definite. Lesie added to it with a swift, "We might have some interest in a cause here and there, but we remain outside it. Oh yes, we've gone along, especially lately, but only as observers, to see what we can see. Which is just a riot. Very unhelpful from our point of view."

"Why do you continue with any involvement at all in these affairs when you realise they're leading to trouble?" Shields demanded brusquely.

For a minute the younger men seemed to be speaking silently to one another over Shields' grey head, then Lesie said shortly, "We're irked. You could say that. Or that we feel we're being challenged. We've kept on because we want to pinpoint the source of trouble."

"Besides," the bearded face on Shields' other side came closer to him, as the man leaned forward, "there's the fact that if we didn't go ahead someone else would do it. The demonstrations are going on and on, just so long as there are things to protest about, and injustices and cruelty. We wash our hands of it and perhaps someone who's a lot less good at organisation than us takes over, and things get worse."

There was mockery in Lesie's soft added, "Besides, our income's cut. There's crude facts for you, Mr. Shields. Money is a dirty subject, but oh, isn't it a lovely one!" The mockery grew, along with the man's smile. "Lovely, lovely money and though few of us admit it, lovely, lovely money is what matters to us most. You yourself, for instance—you don't kid yourself, do you, that you solve puzzles and problems just to help people. There's lovely, lovely money involved.

"There you have it. You know we've had the police round here so many times we've lost count. Sometimes in their dear blue uniforms and official boots, and sometimes in civvies, looking all jolly and out-on-the-town, and pretending they hardly know what the word Cop means. It's really hilariously funny, but you get so damned sick of it, because they're incapable of believing we're a perfectly simple pair of blokes who just like lovely, lovely money.

"They think there's some deep, dark, nasty, putrid reason we're hiding away from them. Like I said," he pulled a face, "they're tiresome, yet you can't help laughing at them.

"The fact is, there's money in it and to my mind it's just a job, as honest as any other. An estate agent does a job, and an advertising man does a job, and a salesman does a job, and what about it? It's honest work and nobody looks sideways because sometimes the houses might be shoddy in the extreme, or the thing being advertised is worthless, or the salesman is setting a real bomb of a car in front of you.

"It's that way with us. We're doing a job. Sometimes we might personally think the causes are crazy, but still ... so long as others think it's genuine, we'll help. We give value for the cash expended, too. Don't doubt it. And it's a lot of hard work, though we have it down to comparative routine by now."

"Who pays you?" Shields pressed bluntly. "The Communist party?" His gaze was on Bratton.

Both of them laughed outright. Lesie said lightly, "Oh lor, that old bogie! Sure, Rex's a Commie, but what's that mean today? Precious little. There's Socialism, at least, in nearly everything—the welfare benefits, the amenities employees take for granted, in education, even in taxes. Anyway the old tub-thumping Commie's right out of date. You've only to look at Russia today—with a new aristocracy in place of the old. Now it's the scientists and the sportsmen, the artists ... oh hell," he laughed again, "now you have *me* tub-thumping.

"No, there's nothing political. Anyway, Rex and I wouldn't see agreement on that point. If he's well to the Left, I'm well over in the opposite direction. The only political area we're likely to meet on, and help, without coming to verbal blows, is the middle of the road one!"

The laughter, the glances between the two, was gay, half mocking, yet Jefferson Shields was again reminded of the patter of two showmen.

Lesie went on, "I know the police suspect it. Politics, I mean. They keep looking at Rex as though they're trying to see horns, and I wouldn't be surprised if one day I'm not asked to remove my socks so they can see my cloven feet.

"No, look..." he leaned forward earnestly, the light shining on the spectacles, so that his eyes were hidden. "We're approached by some group with a cause they want to bring to public notice. Good. We charge a small fee, initially, for introducing them to other groups with the same aims.

"That's how we began. I suddenly thought how stupid it was that there's one demonstration somewhere for something and another for almost the same purpose the next day somewhere else, and again in yet another place a week later—all rag-tag and bobtail—all small, disorganised meetings that fail to draw any attention worth the trouble. I thought they needed bringing together, welding into something that would really make people think.

"For one example: I might be approached by a group of people wanting a council or government decision rescinded, because unless it is they're going to have something like an unpleasant industry dumped in their district.

"We contact another area that has suffered similar invasion. They're invited along to give expression as to how their district has suffered.

"If architects have spoken out against the plan we can draw in the architectural students, and they're sure to bring in others who'll support them."

"Do you always try to bring in student groups?"

"Well ... yes. A lot of working adults just can't spare the loss of wages, the time, and the kids can cut lectures if they're really interested. Then they're more earnest, more receptive, more..."

"Malleable?" Shields suggested dryly, to be cut down with a sharp:

"The donkey you lead to water doesn't have to drink it if he's not inclined—and no, I don't consider them donkeys, fools—that just puts facts into sketchy words, that's all."

He drew a deep breath. "Well then, if there'll be possible air pollution the people interested in that will always jump in with both feet; if there's going to be noise, the various noise-abatement societies will be interested. If there's danger of heavy and considerable traffic past schools for instance, we can get the support of teachers and parents and so on.

"You see..." he was smiling, "there's no end really to the number of people you can draw on if you have file-cards of all these societies and groups and that's only a small example I've given you. Most of the causes involve deeper, more important issues—conscription, war, racist, unpopular governmental decisions—dozens of things.

"The fact is, the first group might have the basis of a small fighting fund. If they went at it by themselves they might, with a lot of work, gather together others interested, who'll help them. If, on the other hand, they give us the fighting fund, we'll bring in everyone who can help, we'll have signs printed at cut rates, we'll distribute them cheaply through volunteers from various other groups, and we'll arrange a march, a demonstration, speeches—the whole works."

He leaned back. He said, "We're just an agency, that's all, and like any agency we can't be responsible for outsiders. Look, can the estate agent be responsible for someone coming and smashing your windows in as soon as you've bought a house off him and moved in? Of course not. If he's tried to find you a decent area, how can he be blamed for an outsider coming in and smashing your peace? And the advertising man? Is he responsible for the hooligans who deface the advertising hoardings? Or the car salesman? Is he responsible if, five minutes after you've bought a car off him, some kid pinches it and smashes it to pieces?"

He said flatly, "We're carrying blame we shouldn't have to shoulder. I've said we've laughed at the cops hanging around, but we resent it, too. Bitterly. I hope you have more sense. I hope you'll accept what I've told you. Do you?" he challenged.

Mildly Shields agreed, "I certainly accept that you, and the estate agent, and the car salesman and the advertising man are not responsible for outside influences."

There was a grunt of laughter from Rex Bratton. He said softly, "I think he's a bit of a tricky bastard. These kids," his gaze slid sideways to the girl, "have put you on to finding out who the outsiders are so they can dodge from under over Robyn Calder's death. Do you think you're going to get any place on that caper?"

"Did you know Robyn Calder?" was the only response.

Lesie was frowning as he said shortly, "No. Of course she might have come here some time. We certainly had no personal contact with her."

"Not even through the demonstrations?"

"No. I imagine she attended the meetings and listened to our instructions. She'd know us, of course. Naturally we've talked about it, but to the best of our belief we've never spoken personally to her. Why? Do you imagine the girl knew about this arming?" He stated bluntly, "There's a whisper going around about a photo—that she was caught by a camera at the wrong moment, when she was armed."

Shields didn't answer directly. He said, "If that were so I should imagine it would be a case of that other person you mentioned—something was thrust into her hand and she thought that if arming was going on, she was going to protect herself. She was afraid of violence. Very much afraid."

Lesie thought that over, then nodded. "I expect that's what it boils down to. The next step is obvious. In a mob like that you see someone armed and you think—That for a game!—and you wrench it off them, and give them a good whack as a warning to mend their manners. That's what it boils down to, doesn't it?"

"Or the fact," Shields suggested gently, "that she was murdered—followed into that crowd, and deliberately killed. Perhaps she had learned something inconvenient. Tell me, did Oliver Harrap come here?"

"Yes." The answer was given before Lesie had time to think, then his mouth snapped shut.

"You knew him well?" Shields pressed.

"A bit," this time the answer was delayed.

"He came here with other men who were conscientious objectors?"

The two younger men were looking at one another. Lesie answered without looking away from Bratton, "Yes."

"Did you ever organise a demonstration for them?"

"Yes." Lesie was still not looking at him.

Shields was on his feet. He said placidly, "I shan't take up more of your time. It was very good of you to chat for so long." His glance urged the girl to her feet, to follow after him.

Only when they were close to the louvred doors at the end of the passage did Lesie move and come after them, and then he merely unlocked the door into the clubroom with a curt, "Your table's been reserved for you," and the door clicked shut behind them.

Chris Stowe linked her arm through Shields'. She asked, "Why did you say that? You've already told us we've wasted your time. You'd discarded the idea of murder, or it seemed so and yet now ... do you mean she could have found out, through knowing Oliver and his friends, getting involved with one in particular, that she could have found out who was doing all this ... this sabotaging, as they call it?"

"It *is* an idea," he pointed out placidly. He asked, "Do you want to stay on?" When she shook her head, he said, "Then I would like to speak to this Graham Whitty—the last student to see her alive."

"Mr. Shields," her hand was dragging on his arm, slowing his steps towards the doorway, "what did you really have in mind..."

Almost brusquely he said, "I was putting a starved cat into the pigeon cage. I," he informed her, "am in the position of the starved cat, you might say. It will be interesting to see what comes of my suggestion. It was apparent I startled and upset them. Perhaps it was simply that they were presented with an unpleasant idea. Perhaps not ... can you get hold of this Graham Whitty?"

Her hand dropped away. He had angered her again, he knew quite well. She said shortly, "He might be home, or he might not be. I can ring and see." The offer was made ungraciously, but his acceptance of it was as placid as ever.

CHAPTER TEN

An overgrown schoolboy might have been the tag applied to Graham Whitty, until the observer looked beyond the obvious facts that the six-foot, heavily built frame was still carried awkwardly, uneasily, with the ungrace of adolescence, and that the skin was pimpled and pitted.

At first he had been almost inarticulate, obviously feeling an unease close to panic. He sat nervously, awkwardly, legs sprawled, big hands clenching together convulsively, and relaxing, only to clench tightly once more, his gaze darting anywhere but the older man's face.

Jefferson Shields had politely, but quite definitely, handed the girl into a taxi outside the Thought Club, and as definitely had told her, "If I need you I'll call you," before he had taken another taxi to the northern suburb that was Whitty's home.

The house had been a surprise—a long, sprawling, and gracious place, with a view from the wide windows that had enchanted Shields immediately he had been ushered into the room.

The boy had made no effort to draw the blinds down, though in the brilliantly lighted room they must have stood out clearly for anyone outside to see.

Whitty burst out at last, "It's quite true. Absolutely true. It happened to me once, so I can tell you it's absolutely true. There was this mix-up and I was wondering if I was going to lose my duds and my skin and even my pimples," he suddenly looked full at Shields and grinned at him derisively, in self-mockery and with the grin, seemed to relax, settling further back in the chair as he went on, "and then this voice yelled in my ear, 'Take this!' You just couldn't stop yourself doing exactly that. Well, I couldn't anyway, and it was fully a couple of minutes before I had a real look—even a chance to look—at what I'd been given.

"It was like facing a tiger snake," he said simply. "I know I yelled out loud, because all I could think of was, Holy Cheese, if I'm caught with this I'm done for, and I was sweating like mad at the mere thought of what might happen. I just dropped it, as fast as I'd taken it and I moved away from the damn thing fast, too, before I was pulled out of the crowd by the police. I didn't want to be found anywhere near the damn thing, I can tell you.

"For a week afterwards," he admitted with another of those self-mocking grins, "I sat around chewing my nails off, reckoning the police would have it and would have my prints off it and any minute they'd roll round the front door and ask me politely for a look at my prints.

"Believe me," he said with real feeling, "I went through hell that week, but nothing happened."

"Did you tell anyone about this?"

"No. Does that sound weird? When you think about it closely," he urged, "it won't seem so. You take a place like University and you blab something, and before it's been five minutes off your tongue it's circling the whole place—with embellishments.

"If I'd said to someone, 'Look, in that bunrush someone shoved a lead bar into my hand'—in five minutes the word would have been bouncing back from every wall in the place that G. Whitty had been armed in that crush. What happens next? The tutors hear it, the University board hears it, the police hear it and what happens to G. Whitty? He's on the bare boards being asked a few hard questions. It's all very well to claim all I had to do was to tell the truth, but what's to say they'll believe it? The fact is I've admitted I was armed, and if anyone in that mêlée was hurt, well ... and in point of fact, in that particular one someone was hit and got a cracked collar bone. Hit, mind you, by something nasty, like a bit of lead piping. If anyone was going to hear that G. Whitty had been playing with just such an item, G. Whitty was in trouble.

"That's how I looked at it, so I kept my mouth shut."

"Do you think that other students have had the same experience?" Shields asked.

The boy seemed quite relaxed now. His dark head was back against the cushioned back of the chair. He said without hesitation, "I rather expect so. I've thought about that question quite a lot since it happened to me, and I honestly can't imagine I'm the only one, and I reckon they'd all do what I did. They'd find themselves armed and police and photographers only a gasp away, and they'd drop whatever it was like a hot coal and just run—*and* shut up about it in case any blame for any damage was tossed into their lap. You see, sir, there's trouble of one sort or another at nearly all these shows lately. Unpleasant, but true, and the trouble's not coming from us." His mouth had firmed, and so had his voice, "It's coming from outside somewhere, but the point is, we nearly always collar the blame. Those Blanky-Blanky Kids, that's the catch-cry. When you have that sort of attitude thrust up your nose you don't go begging for trouble to land on your head as well. You don't go around burbling that in such and such a demonstration you were lugging around a cosh, a piece of bicycle chain, a bit of gas piping, or anything else like it. If you did there'd be someone to yip you'd hurt someone, or damaged property, or started the riot—anything they cared to throw at you, and the claim might be made to stick.

"What could you throw back at them?" He shrugged. "Not a thing. You'd be nicely in a corner. Yes, quite honestly, I do think others have nearly been caught the way I nearly was. It doesn't seem sense to do a thing like that, except you realise someone wants to bring your cause, your argument, the purpose of the demonstration, into disrepute. It makes you sick," he added frankly.

"Nothing more?" Shields suggested. "Just that one reason? You can't think of any others?"

The boy was frowning. He admitted at last, "No. None I can see as reasonable. Are you thinking of hooligans? The bash and bang brigade who just like bashing for fun?"

116

"That, among others. Inspector Virtue ... have you met him?"

"Oh—oh, have I!" The dark eyes rolled expressively.

Shields didn't smile. He said reflectively, "He has nightmares. So he tells me. About these demonstrations being used as a background to organised crime. Centre a demonstration and have all attention, and all available police, centred there, and rob a bank, a big jewellery store, elsewhere. Organise your demonstration to a site, and a time, that suits yourself. Have you considered that?"

"Well now, I don't consider that possible at all." The answer came with assurance and without hesitation. At the quick surprised raising of the grey brows, Whitty added: "There was quite a beef in the correspondence columns of the press some time ago. You know the sort of letters— blah-blah-blast—all about students and signed by Mother of Five, and War Service and Justice and all the rest of them. Among other things that very suggestion was made. In fact, more than you've said—it was made out we were actually being used right then.

"We had an open forum on it among ourselves and went to work to disprove the idea. The police were jolly co-operative that time. We pinpointed all the recent big crimes, proved quite conclusively that out of dozens of demonstrations, only one had taken place when a big crime job had taken place. All the rest of the jobs were just petty stuff —the pinching from offices left vacant for ten minutes or so. You can hardly blame student demonstrations for people acting like fools and leaving their valuables about to be pinched, to my mind.

"We wrote a letter to the same paper that'd printed the others." Bitterly he added, "They never printed it, or so much as acknowledged it. We did ask about it later. We had an answer that we'd waited too long and that correspondence about the demonstrations had now ceased. There was no point in bucking—we had to let it slide.

"The point I'm trying to make is, that if public thought started linking big crime and demonstrations, the whole purpose of using the demonstrations as a front would just collapse—bang, phft! You'd need only three or four jobs and somebody to notice the coincidence and next time there was a demonstration you wouldn't be able to get near a bank or a jewel store or something like that without half the police force breathing down your neck and asking you to come take a little walk.

"Now that's reason, isn't it?"

"Yes," Shields agreed. "You've made your point."

Half in embarrassment Whitty confessed, "You're easy to talk to. I'm quite enjoying this—now. I was scared green when you first came. Why *did* you come?"

"To ask you about the day Robyn Calder died." At the little grimace he added, "I know you must have been over your story endlessly, but I want to hear it again. She was tossed on top of you?"

"Yes, that's so. Woof!" He pressed his hands to his stomach. "She wasn't big, but she felt like a brick wall. She shrieked like a banshee too."

"And what followed?"

"I tried lobbing her off, and she clutched me to keep from going on her back." He grinned again. "For about a minute we must have looked like a pair of lovers playing games that don't belong in the parlour."

"She clutched you—with both hands? She wasn't carrying anything?"

"No. Is it true that she was armed? That there's actually a photo." He said soberly, "I told you you've only to whisper something near a University and the whole place is shrieking the news in five minutes. Is it true?"

"Yes."

"Then I'll tell you quite definitely and honestly that she wasn't armed when she fell on me. I'm positive of it. Her hands were empty. She was wearing slacks and a jersey and a jacket, and I had my arms tight around her. If there'd been anything like an iron bar—that's the rumour as to what she had." He looked up questioningly, and at the other's nod he went on, "If there'd been anything I would have felt it, because someone reached down and grabbed at her hair and tried to pull her up. It was a woman who did that. She was livid. Robyn'd been kicking out, trying to get upright and she must have copped the woman a bash on the ankle I expect. It's difficult to tell just what does happen in those affairs. But the woman grabbed her hair that way—it was just a yank, no real power in it, but I wrapped my arms tight round her to save her being jerked back. Look—there wasn't anything but Robyn in my hands. She was only thin. I reckon she wasn't even wearing so much as a bra."

He shook his head. He said soberly, "She must have been caught the way I was that other time, don't you think? That throws the blame on me, doesn't it? I should have spoken out that other time, so we'd all have been warned."

"And what would all of you have done if you had been given a warning?"

Whitty hesitated, then admitted, "Nothing, I suppose. You'd say to yourself, well if it happens to me I'll make sure I get a look at this fellow, but in a fight ... in a crowd ... there'd be one startled second, of course, when you clutched at whatever it was and tried to turn and keep your wits all at the same time and by then whoever it was would have turned his back and be shoving away from you. How'd you be able to put a finger on the right chap? You couldn't, could you?"

Dryly Shields pointed out, "You have experience of these demonstrations. I have not. Tell me, did you know Robyn Calder well?"

"No. Hardly at all."

"You've no knowledge, real knowledge, that is, of how she might react in a given situation? If..."

"No, unless you count what I've learned since she died. Naturally we've all hashed over everything anyone could say about her. Probably a lot of that is rumour piled on rumour..."

"What, in particular?"

"Oh ... just, she had a mystery man in her life. There's been a lot of speculation about that. It doesn't seem to go with other things I've heard about her—oh," impatient now, he dismissed the subject with a quick, "she was dad-da's girl. That type. A bit of a pure lily. No, I'm not talk-ing about sex. Other things. Wrong is wrong and right is right and never the twain shall meet. It doesn't go with mystery men that she's not game to take home to meet dad. Like I said though, most of it'd be rumour."

It was the boy who broke the silence that had fallen over the room. He said solemnly, "It wasn't fair for her to die that way. I mean, to be killed for something she couldn't help. She gets an iron bar put into her hand. She never *meant* to be armed at all. All right, but she was. So someone sees it and thinks she needs a lesson and grabs it and deals her one. It was so damned unfair."

CHAPTER ELEVEN

Shields was tempted to ask if the Inspector ever relaxed at all. When he had phoned Virtue and been invited to come round, in spite of the hour, to the other man's house, he had expected to find a man considerably different from the soft-voiced, worried-looking man of the police office.

Virtue was still as neatly dressed as he had been earlier in the day, though. It seemed to Shields that the man considered his home as an extension of that hot, small office with its smell of decay underlying new paintwork; that he considered himself always on the job, always ready, even eager to return to it.

The only difference to Shields' welcome, when he arrived at the small brick house in a western suburb, was Virtue offering drinks, and sandwiches.

Shields shook his head to that, explaining, as he let his gaze go slowly round the small sunroom they'd entered, that he had only recently left the Thought Club. Virtue's expression didn't change. He asked only, "How did you like it?"

Shields let him wait while he completed his scrutiny. He found the room curiously depressing. The furniture was too heavy and dark—it drowned the small room, and heavy curtains shut off the two sides that were glassed in. He found his interest sliding away, to a consideration of the kind of man who was content to spend the days of his life between that tiny police office, and attendance on outside crime scenes, and this small house in the quiet suburban backwater.

Only when Virtue asked again, "How did you like it?"

did he force his mind away from the contemplation.

He said simply, "I disliked Lesie and Bratton very much indeed."

Virtue gave a brief nod. There was a faint smile on his mouth, a smile that broadened as he said dryly, "Don't blame me for the furnishings—for this room. It's my landlady's choice." At the other man's quick turn of head, Virtue said shortly, "My marriage crashed a long time ago. I never intend to repeat it. What in particular made you come down for a verdict of dislike?"

"The fact they consider themselves of an intelligence far superior than mine. Yours, too. That sort of attitude is acceptable sometimes, though irritating always, but Lesie and Bratton are so sure of themselves, of that same intelligence, that they find it quite reasonable they should parry me with a set of words, a series of gestures, a hint, an attitude that they have used so many times before they sound like a pair of showmen with what they consider an assured formula for a successful show."

Irritably he went on, "I imagine I'm failing to show you what..."

"No. I think I understand very well. I've had much the same impression. Move on to another question. What did they tell you about this organising?"

"That it was a case of what Lesie calls lovely, lovely money. How much do these fighting funds amount to, that people manage to scrape together? Lesie claims he's told you, the police in general, of..."

"Yes. The money that's handed over varies. Sometimes small, sometimes quite large. Expenses are kept pared to the most economical sum, but I'm not saying that there is anything crooked about that. They don't simply take money under false pretences. The job is always what you'd call value for the money given."

"It would have to be. They wouldn't have lasted so long if they didn't come up to expectations. They would advertise themselves by word of mouth recommendation."

"That's right."

Shields reminded, "And they cannot be held responsible

for an outside element who ruins the organisation—as Lesie points out, with examples of other employment to back up his claim. Now take expenses from the money handed over to them. Tell me what's left."

Virtue grinned. He said, "Nine hundred and thirty-seven dollars. That's what they put on their tax return last year. Oh yes, they're within the law on every point you can think up. They have books showing any amount paid them and every last cent expended, right down to the last stamp and even—don't laugh—a packet of band-aids for an injured helper! They're running a business. They have a registration for it. They keep books that are audited along with the club books. They account for every cent of profit in their tax records and they pay their taxes promptly."

He shot out, "Do you think nine hundred and thirty-seven dollars is a worthwhile profit? Take into account the time they must spend on it—they're not taking salary out of these sums handed to them. Their payment is strictly in the profits. All right, take into account their time, take into account the worry—if they're on the level—about things going wrong. Take every last thing you can dream up into account and tell me, is that profit something you'd call lovely, lovely money when it's divided between the two of them? It's money, that's all, and not much of it."

"How much profit is there in running the Club?"

"Quite good. Quite reasonable, and there they have us again. Ask them if they consider the work and worry of this organising worthwhile and they smile blandly and point out it brings more people to the Club; it helps swell the profits there, that when you add one account to another, the organising gives them a far better profit than it appears to give at first sight.

"So?" He looked expectantly at the other man.

"So you're still doubtful. So am I," Shields admitted. "Consider this point. They claim they have kept on with the organising in the hope of finding out who or what is behind this rioting. They spoke to me of having monitors scrutinise the marchers, the demonstrations, to watch for armed people, to pick them out and question them. They claim only two men have been definitely identified and so questioned."

"Yes, we've heard about that, too. Frank, aren't they? Never a thing hidden from us." His voice was bitter.

"Has there been any attempt to have these demonstrations filmed? To have still photography? To..."

Virtue grinned. He said softly, "They're way ahead of you. We've asked that, too. The answer is simply lovely, lovely money. Have you ever considered the cost of filming just one show? No, they're quite right there—the cost would be so excessive it would be impossible. Anyway how could you have cameras, still or movie, focused on every point? You'll get men like Morrow to take shots he thinks will be interesting and profitable, but ... you'd need an army of cameras to cover a whole demonstration riot. Cost again, even if you could find men willing to wade into the job, with the risk they or the cameras would be smashed up.

"No, on the face of it, they've done all they could possibly do with the funds available to them."

"Morrow has photographed a considerable number..."

"None that could be used for positive identification. Yes, I pulled him in after speaking to you. He's agreed to shut up about his hobby-horse. Did Lesie, or Bratton, tell you there's another demonstration tomorrow, near Hyde Park?"

"No?" When Virtue didn't answer the question in the denial, Shields went on to speak of Graham Whitty and to add, "I asked him if he had ever considered the possibility that these affairs could be used for organised crime."

Virtue's hand, reaching for another cigarette from the Japanese lacquer box on the table between them, became still. He lifted his gaze to the other man. He asked, "Well?" without inflection, but he made no move to complete taking the cigarette. Instead he snapped the box shut and leaned back in his chair, waiting.

"He gave me extremely good arguments against the possibility. He's right, you know—the project would defeat itself in very short order. People—ordinary people—or as Morrow might say, you and me and Tom Brown and Uncle

Joe—aren't interested very much in factories and what happens in them. It is a different matter with the theft of jewels, with a bank hold-up. The public imagination, and envy, is aroused. There is a Ned Kelly in the best of us who secretly admires the men who can gain a fortune with a daring robbery. Such an event would gain more prominence, I should imagine, than violent demonstrations. Put three, four, five such days, with a demonstration and a big robbery taking place together and just as Whitty points out, the general public would sit up and take notice and next time there was a demonstration all the banks would be so armed and watchful it would be dangerous to enter them!"

Virtue's, "Three, four, five," was bitter, angry and violent. He jumped to his feet, went over to the desk in the corner, opened it and came back with a flat folder in his hand, spreading it open, on the table close to Shields.

He pointed down at the map revealed. He said curtly, "There's the city. The whole wide city," his finger slowly traced the outlines of it on the map. "There's Hyde Park," his finger stopped, "where tomorrow's demonstration—this time over the conscription business again—is going to take place.

"Now, look here," his finger moved, a little to one side, and again to another point and once more to a third. "They're streets close by and in each of those streets or arcades leading off them there are jewellers and each of those places are small and out of the way—some upstairs—and each of them carries a great deal of easily portable wealth.

"Have your demonstration, bring it to the boiling point of violence and all the city's attention is right there," his finger stabbed, "and all the police who can be sent are there trying to control things. Then have two men here," his finger moved, "and two here, and two more there, and two or three beyond and another two over there. Don't look so doubtful, Shields. Think of England's great train robbery for a start—how many men were involved in that? Picture those men, organised and ready and waiting. They move in, on those small, isolated and unprotected jewellers. Oh yes, certainly they wouldn't hesitate to use violence. Why not? Once you couldn't carry a gun without risk of real punishment—now the law's so mild that it's matter of course to be armed and to use it to make sure you get away safely. In fifteen minutes, or even much less, a small fortune could be swept out of the city."

He said with that anger and bitterness back in his voice, "That's one job. Just *one*. And you speak of three, four, five—think of all of them organised like that, and you'll realise why I have nightmares. Two jobs alone would be sufficient to set any gang up for a lifetime of ease. Then it would cease, just until another gang got themselves organised and set to work."

Shields asked sharply, "Are you expecting something of this sort to happen tomorrow? Is that—"

There was a jerk of laughter. Virtue was refolding the map as he said, "As the old saying goes, I hope for the best and expect the worst. No, I'm not more suspicious, more anxious, than at any other time."

"Whitty claims the students drew up a letter to the press showing the incidence of crime during demonstrations and they pointed out the majority were merely petty crime. He says the police co-operated in giving records."

"That's so. The district men sent in reports, requests for approval for handing out the facts. It all reached my desk finally. Most things do. I've kept the lists flowing in to keep an eye on the extent of it, and make sure the pros. aren't moving in, but it's just as I said before—petty, most of it local. The culprit's usually someone working in the building. There's a lot of risk involved in a stranger walking through offices, but not for someone from an office who knows who's likely to be inside, or not. Anyway, if he's caught he has only to say he was looking for someone and why should they be suspicious? By the time they've discovered they've been robbed he's been to the washroom and unloaded his pockets and there's nothing to pin on him. You can see the lists if you wish."

Shields nodded acceptance of the offer, but he asked, "Do you think there'll be a fire tomorrow?"

"Yes. Depends, of course, on the weather for one thing, because a day of full rain is no good for a fire. There'll be violence tomorrow though. These conscription marches invariably attract it. There'll be the followers who rant at the placards, abuse the marchers, claim the whole thing's an insult—oh, work it out for yourself!"

Shields asked, "What happens to these demonstrations if there is a downpour?"

"Sometimes they're cancelled at the last minute, or there's an alternative indoor site chosen. Depends." He shrugged. "I've known them cancelled even if it looks like rain."

"So at times it wouldn't be known, until the last minute, whether the demonstration mightn't be moved elsewhere?"

"I know what you're thinking. There'd have to be some means of letting the arsonists know if the site's changed, or the whole thing cancelled, or they might start a fire where the brigades could reach them in minutes and the job would be spoilt. Most factories now have phone calls to their staff monitored. There's a record of every phone call taken, during the time of a demonstration in the city. It applies to the factories who've been hit by wild-cat strikes, too. Don't you realise," he asked harshly, "that we've had months of this—months to talk and to thrash things out and to realise how bad it is, and months to go over every last point..." He stopped. He added flatly, "The monitoring hasn't got us anywhere.

"We're positive there has to be some way the factories know whether to go ahead with the arson. That's another pointer, by the way, to manual starting of the fires.

"It isn't only the weather, you see. There are other factors. There could be an accident. If it's bad it can block a whole sector of the city. Any demonstration headed for it would have to detour elsewhere or disband. There are other things, too—a water main can burst and cut off a street. Electricity cables can break. Machines and workmen can take over a whole area. There are dozens of reasons why a march has a detour elsewhere at the last minute. We've even headed them off ourselves if we expected bad trouble and they were approaching an over-crowded part of the city. There needs to be some way an arsonist in these factories knows that the march is going ahead as planned, that certain streets will be blocked by it, making the fire brigades late reaching the fire scene, and that the police forces are already having too much to attend to."

He slammed the desk shut on the refolded map and came back to his chair. He went on, more slowly, "Monitoring of phones hasn't helped. We've considered a radio signal. With all these transistors about, taking a radio on to the job is easy, but you couldn't have an ordinary one— it would have to be something capable of receiving an outside signal. You could be caught out too easily—someone else could pick it up and discover it wasn't what it seemed.

"We've even come down to considering hearing aids. I don't know what the poor devils wearing them have thought of the sudden interest in their hearing, but they've all been scooped up, on the grounds of factory welfare and special tests that might help them.

"All we found," the admission was rueful, "was an amazing incidence of deaf people in factories. So we come down to something that looks nothing like a radio and we're helpless. How can you search every employee, every day, of every factory that might be hit?"

"Have you searched *outside* the factory?" When Virtue turned, frowning, waiting, the other man went on, "Have you searched outside for a van—a delivery van that has honest business in the factory itself? They often carry two-way radios for contact with their home base. Have you thought they can call or not call at a factory and call at a time whenever they choose? In these days of clogged roads, deliveries can be early or late. Have you thought that if a van—a bright, easily seen van—went into a factory yard it might well be a signal to someone inside to go ahead with a planned job? If it didn't come..."

He added, "A repair van would be suspect too. Repairmen never call on time and come and go as they choose. The only requirement would be that it could be easily seen by someone in the factory or office inside. It *is* possible, isn't it?" he suggested almost diffidently, in the face of the continued silence.

It was Shields who finally broke the silence with the suggestion, "It would take only one man to each factory you considered vulnerable to watch for a parked lorry or repair van and alert you, and if it moved suddenly into the factory yard, to alert the factory's security. With a little co-ordination everywhere it would be possible in a very short time to watch for the sudden movement of any employee, on whatever excuse, to another part of the building."

He wasn't prepared for the tight anger that was close to sheer blinding rage, in the other's face, or his barked, "Who's mentioned that set-up to you?"

After a moment Shields offered, "It was simply going to see young Whitty. No," he denied sharply, "it doesn't involve him in what we were discussing. It was simply that I was told his father was a refrigeration mechanic, which is an occupation I hadn't connected with considerable reward. The house was a vast surprise, then I realised that Whitty senior was not a one-man concern, but a company. There was a van parked near the driveway, with D. Whitty & Associates printed on it. I was thinking, as I waited for the doorbell to be answered, how distinctive the van appeared and I was reading the information, 'Radio controlled for immediate service'.

"When you spoke now of radios the thought just came into my head. No one has brought my attention to it. Why?"

"I imagined someone might have talked out of turn." Without further comment on the point he demanded, "Did you mention this business of fires and strikes there—at the Thought Club I mean?"

"No. I did, however, ask if Oliver Harrap had ever been to the place?"

"Harrap?" Virtue's voice went up in astonishment. "The Conshie? Where's the point in . . ."

"I wanted to know if he was in the habit of going there, with friends who were conscientious objectors. I wanted to know if Robyn Calder had been there, also. Lesie said yes, to the first two questions and no, so far as he was aware, to the second."

Virtue was frowning, eyes intent. "Where's the point of the questions?"

"Simply that the question of this man, this stranger, continues to nag at me," Shields admitted. "I wondered if the man could have been a conscientious objector, who was jailed, as was Harrap. Harrap's girlfriend, who happens to be my secretary, Ann Aveyard, was placed in a difficult position with her family because of his behaviour. I wondered if the same thing had applied to the Calder girl. Her father, according to others who have heard him on the subject, considers there are only two types of men in the world—those who do their duty; those who do not and are cowards and traitors. The girl might have found life impossible at home if she had confessed to taking up with a traitor, a coward, a jail-bird."

Virtue dismissed the idea with a shrug, and a brief, "It hardly matters, does it?"

"Perhaps not, except as a means of bringing Robyn Calder's name into the conversation with Lesie and Bratton."

"And why should you do that?" Virtue sounded abstracted now, as though his thoughts had left both the conversation and his visitor and were on other things.

"To give a good stir to whatever pot is boiling there," Jefferson Shields told him. "I wanted to bring those two from their smug satisfaction and make them do something —anything at all except sit there and laugh at me. I asked if she had been there, and had been in the organising of these demonstrations. I suggested that for all anyone knew the girl might have been deliberately killed, because she had found out something she wasn't supposed to know."

Now Virtue's attention was fully caught again. He stared, then burst out laughing. "You've a damn cool hide!" he burst out, then asked in real curiosity, "What did they say to it?"

"Remarkably little, but I was shown out with a speed at variance with their manner up to then, which had been casual and leisurely and very much at ease. I gave them

130

something to think about. If there's something going on they don't wish made public, they'll be thinking very hard now, about the possibility that the Club will come under a too public scrutiny between now and the Inquest.

"I rather think that my first caller in the morning will be one of that pair—or perhaps, both."

Virtue mocked, "Knowing so much—what are they going to say? Tell me that."

Shields shook his head. "Whatever it is, it should prove interesting, and one thing—" his voice expressed complete satisfaction in the reflection, "they should spend an uneasy night." He asked curtly, "Why did you imagine someone had talked to me of a van being used as a signal?"

Virtue's body jerked. His half-smile vanished. He began, curtly, "We're working on that line. Leave it," then abruptly he shook his head, and began to speak again.

CHAPTER TWELVE

The first caller of the day wasn't either Lesie or Bratton. It was Alexander Calder whom Ann ushered into the inner office.

In the khaki uniform that, along with their job of dropping on illegally parked cars, had earned the parking police the nickname of Brown Bombers, and with his uniform cap still on his head, he looked younger, and almost unrecognisable as the untidy, shirt-sleeved man of the previous evening.

His manner was more assured, too, as he flipped the uniform cap on to Shields' desk and took the visitors' chair without waiting to be asked. He said bluntly, "I had the press round the place last night."

"Why?"

"That photo of Robyn. Were you the one who told?" At the shake of the grey head, Calder went on crisply, "Well, it seems to be public knowledge, or at least, there are enough rumours flying to make a flock of bats look small. The police told me, when they *did* tell me—and that was long after I should have known, in my own opinion—not to let it out. I don't know why exactly. I just obeyed orders. Now all of a sudden, it's public property and I had the press back on my doorstep wanting to know if it was true and what about it, if so." He added, "I referred them to the police. About the photo, that is. As to what I thought about it—that was different. I felt I was quite free to speak my mind, and I did."

He gave a nod to the unvoiced question in the other's face. "You can have what I said. I told them that Robyn was the last girl in the world to have anything to do with arming herself and bashing folk around. I told them

132

what she was—a decent, home-loving, level-headed kid who'd been brought up on ... old-fashioned lines, you'd call it, I expect. I've never given even lip-service to all this permissive business that's all the go." His contemptuous expression told what he thought of the question. He added impatiently, "It's a lot of rot. You've got to bring up a kid to know right from wrong. Right's right, and wrong's wrong. I'd tell her that over and over and she knew it was so.

"Maybe," he hesitated a moment, then admitted, "maybe I sounded a bit too strict. To outsiders. But ... her mother was no good, you see. A real piece of rubbish, the sort who regards a marriage licence as just a licence to get everything they can get out of one man while kicking up their heels with every other pair of trousers that came along.

"We—the wife and I—we wanted Robyn to see, without any argument about it, that stealing another woman's man is as bad as stealing her purse. That's what Robyn's mother did, you see—ran off with someone else's husband and left the woman to bring up two kids on her own. The way my brother was left with Robyn. Well, he was sick then. He got TB in the war and never got over it and he passed out, but a good while before that he asked us to take Robyn.

"We never regretted it. I told those pressmen that last night. We never regretted it. We were proud of her. She was clever, you know. Won a Commonwealth Scholarship and everything to help her go on to University. She wanted to get her BA and go on to doing Social Welfare work. Now I ask you, does that sound like someone who'd deliberately take up a weapon and go around smashing up property and people?"

"No, and I am fairly certain that at the inquest the fact will emerge that these demonstrations were sabotaged, deliberately. There were two occasions at least when a demonstrator in the press of a crowd heard a voice say, 'Take that!' and something was thrust into his hand. By the time he had realised he was armed, the speaker had vanished among the crowd, so that he couldn't pinpoint blame, and indeed would have faced blame himself if it had come out he

133

himself had been armed.

"Tell me, Mr. Calder—this last demonstration. Cast your mind back to the days previous to that demonstration and her death." He saw the blankness, the withdrawal, in the other's face and added sharply, "I know you dislike thinking of it, but I want you to take your mind back to those last days, just the same.

"This demonstration—did you know the purpose of it?"

"Yes. It was a call to release some—I've forgotten his name, but he was a Conshie." His tone held utter distaste for the word.

"You've no sympathy with objectors, have you?"

"Not a particle," the answer came without hesitation. "They talk a lot of bilge, wailing about having their lives interrupted and God knows what. You and me—we fought in that last war. It interrupted your life, I bet. It interrupted mine, plenty. I was a POW for eighteen months, as well as everything else. If we could do it, why can't these kids today?"

Shields gave a little grimace. He brushed the question aside with, "Arguments for and against are not my province. We'll go back to the fact that you have no sympathy with men like Oliver Harrap. What was your attitude then, to your daughter mixing herself up in a demonstration calling for support of his actions?"

Calder took a little time over answering. He said at last, "I was ... furious. Yes, you could say that. I don't like thinking about that now. I didn't usually get mad with her, but that time—it seemed so senseless, you get it? I remember pointing out to her that it was near the end of the term and she'd been saying only a while before that she wished the day had thirty-six hours because she needed more studying time. Yet here she was—and I'd taken a lot of the housekeeping off her shoulders, mind you, so she'd get extra study time—wasting time on something and someone who was just worthless.

"I reminded her of all that, but she was stubborn. She reckoned it wasn't so much his ideas she was ranking herself with, as the cock-eyedness of jailing someone like Har-

134

rap, and throwing him in with a bunch of murderers and thieves and sex maniacs and tricksters and so on.

"Well ... I just don't know. It does seem a bit scatty," he admitted helplessly. "I mean, what's the point? Like she asked me, find me the point? She kept on arguing, bringing up points like it was simply costing the taxpayers good money in keeping him in there, and saying the Government should have some form of peaceable service for people like Harrap—you know all the old arguments that get trotted out in a case where a Conshie tries bucking the ship."

"You didn't *forbid* her to go? You didn't demand that she stay away from the demonstration?"

"No." After a while he added to the bald denial a slow, "She was growing up, you see, and ... well, maybe I was a bit scared. I didn't want her ever to express open defiance of me ... oh well, perhaps though..."

"She was afraid of violence, of being hurt?"

"Yes." He added sharply, "She was no coward though."

"But if a weapon was thrust into her hand, in the middle of a riot, she'd be more likely than most people, to retain her hold of it?"

"Maybe so." He asked abruptly, "They ... at the inquest, it's going to seem she brought it on herself, isn't it? That it wouldn't have happened at all if she'd not held on to that bar. So it comes down to this—whoever does this sabotaging as you call it, killed her. Whoever shoved that bar into her hand killed as though they'd hit her themselves. That's what I came to see you about. I had all night to think, after you'd gone and the press had and I could see what turn things were going to take, so I came here. I want to know who gave her that bar."

He stood up, picking up the uniform cap, standing there to move it slowly round and round between his hands. He said shortly, "You find out who went and armed her, Mr. Shields. You concentrate on that. I want to know." He half turned, then moved back to add, "I can pay you."

Shields said curtly, "I already have a client." He nearly added, "I wish I hadn't."

.   .   .

Deliberately Shields kept his face quite blank, so that there was only indifference in the answer to the challenging, "You intended me to come here, didn't you?" that Athol Lesie threw at him as he strode into the office, brushing aside Ann Aveyard with the impatience of his arrival.

Shields said, "If you felt that, why didn't you want to deny me the pleasure of being proved right?"

It stopped Lesie. He hesitated, then abruptly sat down in the grey chair the other side of the desk, crossed his legs and brought out a cigarette pack, taking his time over the lighting of the cigarette.

He said at last, "Well, well. And well indeed and again. So I've been caught short, made to look a fool, made to feel I've started off on the wrong foot. As Rex said last night, I think you're a tricky bastard."

He suddenly flashed a smile at the older man. He said lightly, "You know, your statement last night was distinctly defamatory. You suggested, quite blatantly so, that there's something distinctly, well odorous, of the nature of a five day kipper, about the Club—so much so that dear little Robyn Calder stuck her small nose round the wrong corner, took a sniff too long and was whacked on the head to teach her nice girls don't sniff other folks' garbage cans."

He moved impatiently. The laughter and mockery was gone. He said flatly, "I don't think you believe so for a minute. You threw that at us to ... stampede us? Into doing what? You must have had something in mind. What?" When there was no answer, a hint of desperation showed under the impatience and anger, "Whatever you're thinking it's not going to do you—or Rex and I either—a scrap of good unless it's brought into the open and we all thrash it out. What's the use of you sitting there glooming at me, filled with suspicion, when all you have to do is open up and ask, 'Explain this' and tell me what it is. Ask..." His arms were thrown wide, expansively. "Ask, Mr. Shields and you shall receive, as the good book says."

"Have you close acquaintance with the good book?" Shields asked dryly.

The eyes rounded in open astonishment. He burst out, "In the name of … now why the devil ask *that*. Oh well, I said I'd answer. As a matter of fact I went to a church school. So did Rex. Funny that, isn't it? Now he's a big, bad Commie. Why that question?"

"Because I am tired of you and you were obviously going to sit there and chatter at me until I broke my silence."

"Well, well, and well again." He gave a jerk of laughter, but his whole expression spoke of barely controlled anger. He asked, "Is that a hint that I go?"

Shields asked, "What does nine hundred and thirty-seven dollars represent to you and Bratton in terms of luxury and ease and happiness?"

"Oh *God!*" The cigarette described an arc through the air, hitting the desk, as Lesie's arms were thrown wide again. Fastidiously the older man retrieved it, stubbing it out in the black onyx ashtray.

Lesie said, "I see you've talked to the police. It represents —I've told them this, repeatedly—a lot of things that aren't apparent. It represents a lot more trade for the Club for a start, and a lot more trade is a lot more profit. If you're at all reasonable, at all aware of what goes on in the city, you'll know clubs like ours spring up one night and are dying in two months and dead and forgotten six months after they began. I can give you the names of dozens who've gone just that way. It would have been that way with us, but we weren't going to let it. We've sunk a lot of money into the Club. We intend to get it back, with interest, so we've taken on a sideline that *keeps* people coming back, that brings others in, that keeps us a live, and an interesting and a needed place.

"Do you judge that as reasonable?"

"Yes. You've made a very good point."

Abruptly Lesie relaxed. Lighting a cigarette he said lightly, "Thank God for an intelligent man, then. The police have resolutely refused to admit it's even faintly reasonable, let alone good."

Gently Shields pointed out, "It in no way invalidates the police suspicion that the Club itself and your organising

137

of these demonstrations is strictly a cover-up for some other activity unstated, and distinctly, as you just put it yourself, of the order of a five day kipper."

The moment of ease had gone. Lesie demanded, "Just what is it you all think we're doing? We've tried every which-way to keep well within the law everywhere. We've..." He said, with an attempt at humour, "Maybe we've tried just a bit too hard, and because we don't sell liquor when we shouldn't; or have a call-girl set-up on the sly; or peddle dope or any of the city's slimier perversions; or run a gambling den in a back room, or pass dud notes, the police think we're too innocent to be true? Or is it sour grapes?" His mouth twisted. "Does some cop find there's no golden handshake for him from us, because there's nothing we have to bribe about, and he doesn't like us for it for cutting his income?"

"Don't be foolish." The retort was tired. "You've talked of defamatory remarks. That was clearly defamatory in the sense you're implying that every other club in the city has been giving the police what you call a golden hand-shake."

"Because no other club is being harassed and questioned and probed at the way we are?" He said triumphantly, "Let's come down now to brass tacks and admit that we're the only club to get this sort of treatment. Why are we?"

"You're well aware of the reason. You are closely involved with these demonstrations and they spell trouble. Almost invariably they cause riots and linked with them, by however coincidental a thread, there are further troubles, both political and criminal."

"Leave aside the political. Apart from Rex belonging to the Communist Party and me belonging to the Young Liberals, we've no truck with politics and you'd never in a thousand years prove we have. Leave that aside and it comes down to crime. So we're supposed to be up to something criminal. What?"

When there was no answer he went on, "I can see where this is heading. Right back to what you threw at us last night. These kids are frightened. Are their parents frightened, too? University students don't as a rule have much money, Mr. Jefferson Shields, and, as I mentioned to you last night, we're all in our little games for lovely money. From what I've heard of you, your services don't come cheaply, so who's paying the bill? The parents, I bet, and some of them would be very well cushioned. Band a few of them together, trying to save their precious brats' hides, with the thought of this inquest coming up next week, and what have you?

"A scream to Mr. Jefferson Shields to do something quick. Never mind who else gets a rap, just so long as the brats save their reputations and skins. So you go looking for a red hot motive that leads right away from student violence and all the rest and you come up with the proposition that Robyn Calder was a nosey little girl who learned a secret.

"You and the parents who've hired you yell 'Murder'. That's fine, but you need to do more than yell to convince the public, so you have to scout round and find a motive. So here comes the hint that maybe all isn't what it seems at the Thought Club. Robyn Calder was mixed up with them, wasn't she, through demonstrations, through her friends going to the Club. What if Robyn found out something about that same Club..."

He stood up, crushing out the half-smoked cigarette with short, savage jabs. He said bluntly, "So now I know where I stand. All right. I walk out of here straight to my solicitor. Try that story in public and I'll soak you for damages from here to Alaska."

.   .   .

When Ann Aveyard's voice said crisply, "It's Inspector Virtue, Mr. Shields," he was tempted to refuse the call; to tell the girl to ask Virtue to ring later, then he said, his mind still on Lesie and Calder and a dozen other things that boiled down to one single person—a dead girl—"Put him through," and immediately Virtue's voice, the softness gone under something approaching shrillness, was saying:
"The march started ten minutes ago. They're going

139

slowly. They got held up because the traffic lights have gone wrong and traffic and pedestrians are all snarled up together."

"And?" Now Shields' attention was on one thing alone —what the other man was saying.

Virtue said, "There's a van—big, distinctive—bright red, with an advertisement on the side for meat pies, near the factory I told you about last night."

Over Virtue's voice going on, "The driver's reading a paper and eating chips. Everything looks like a normal break in his morning's work." Shields was remembering the previous night and the Inspector speaking tiredly of a factory close to the city, whose trade lay in hospital equipment and instruments. He had spoken with a tired certainty of being sure that that factory would be the next hit. Not only because it had recently signed huge contracts with far east interests, but because one main access road to it was already blocked by sewerage main works and a second artery road was narrowed by a building demolition. He had said then, in that same spent voice, "It'd be a natural for a fire if other roads from the city get blocked, too. The brigades will be running round in circles trying to reach it, and look at the position of it," his finger had stabbed at the map. "It should never have been built there, with narrow roads all round it, and terrace houses. A fire will bring everyone out in a minute blocking those roads round it with milling people and furniture they're dragging out in case their homes go."

Shields was remembering that as Virtue now said, "I've contacted the factory. The pie firm has a contract to supply the canteen, but the time the carrier turns up varies a lot—so long as it's before eleven-thirty they don't care."

His voice rose. He said sharply, "Hold on a minute," and time seemed to drag for Shields, then the voice, soft and controlled once more, said in his ear, "The march is moving nicely now. There's nothing to stop it going ahead and there's trouble brewing. Some punches have already been thrown—we've had to move all the police we can spare to that area." Again Shields was hearing the tired voice of the previous evening state, "We'll be busy trying to quell the riot—there'll be no police left to clear the streets round the factory—it's a natural to go up—the whole damn lot of it if once a fire starts tomorrow."

Virtue snapped, "The van's moving!" He said rapidly, "We'll bring the driver in on some traffic breach pretext no matter what happens." His laughter spoke of tension and doubt and excitement. "How handy are our blessed traffic laws! The factory's fully alert now." He stopped. Then, sharper still now the voice asked, "Do you want to come down here? I can't talk any more..."

"I'll come. Thank you."

He was visualising the van as he walked with long strides, a tall, thin, grey figure that was seen and brushed against by hundreds he passed, and as instantly forgotten. He wondered if the driver would come quietly, or fight; whether he would be bewildered, or angry, or frightened or merely sullen.

.   .   .

Denis Ritson was merely indifferent, a little amused, but quite at ease. He said cheerfully, "You'll have to give me a note about this or the boss's going to cut up like the Christmas turkey, about lost time."

He was a small, slim, neat man who might have been about thirty, or might have been middle-aged. The sandy hair and pale eyes and sun-tanned features hid his real age well, along with his quick, almost bouncing walk. In the grey dustcoat over shorts and long socks and white shirt, he might have been any delivery man in the whole city. He went on being quite indifferent as he was shown into the bigger office of the station where he'd been taken, and looked round the circle of faces turning in interest to watch him.

That was wrong. Shields knew that everyone in the room, except Ritson, knew it was wrong. No man, innocent or guilty, was indifferent, when taken abruptly from his job and brought to a police station and confronted by a circle of police.

He should have been asking anxiously, or angrily, why he'd brought this down on himself; why he was there at all. He could even have ranted and talked of his rights and a solicitor and it would still have seemed normal.

Indifference was wrong. As completely wrong as the chirpy way he took the offered chair and accepted a cigarette. He was acting as though the whole set-up was something he met every day in the week, or had expected to meet, one day.

He said brightly, "Well, what's up, chums?" He gave a quick grin upwards at Virtue's face. "You think I've got the notes from the latest bank robbery stuck in m'pies? There might be some funny things in 'em, but nothing that interesting."

He sobered suddenly and seemed to change, as though he was realising for the first time that his chirpiness was overdone. He asked shortly, "Well, what is it? I've played along—so far. Not a squeak out of me, even with you pinching me in full sight, and hearing, of the canteen staff at the factory. 'Just a minute there,' his voice mimicked a low, stolid voice, 'Just a minute. Is that your van parked out there?' And then I'm asked to just come along a minute. It's been a sight longer than a minute already, so it's time for a few explanations."

"We wanted to know why you were parked for seventeen minutes round the corner of the factory, in a side lane." It was Virtue who put the question.

Ritson stared, blew a cloud of smoke, then shrugged. "I can guess something's been busted near the lane. Right?" When there was no answer, he went on, grinning again, "Well don't go saying out loud it was seventeen minutes because I'll only answer to ten. I've a right to that. Ten minutes for refreshments. That's what I was taking. Bought myself ten cents of chips and ate them while I caught up on the news." He half rose. "Now can I go?"

"I'm sorry." Virtue was quite courteous. "Not yet."

Again the simple shrug. Ritson offered, "I didn't see anything, hear anything or do anything, if that's what you're going to ask next."

"It isn't." Virtue's gaze had gone past him, to the doorway behind.

There was another man coming in, flanked by two policemen. He was young and pale, with long dark hair that curled at the back to the collar of his grey overalls. One of the policemen gave him a gentle push so that he moved forward, into Ritson's sight.

There was no expression on either man's face, but tension had entered the room, and again the indifference in the two faces spoke of something wrong. There should have been interest at least, a wonder, a puzzlement.

One of the policemen said, "Thomas Ebeling, sir."

A voice intoned from the back of the room, "He is charged with attempted arson, sir. He was discovered at his place of work setting a fire-making device in a storeroom. Two other devices were found on his person. He has refused any statement."

"Crumbs," Ritson gave a hee-haw of braying laughter, "so'd I in his boots!"

"Do you find arson funny, Mr. Ritson?" was Virtue's soft enquiry.

The laughter died. "Now you mention it, no, but ... what's *he*," he jerked a thumb, "doing in here with *me*?" The thumb jutted towards his own chest.

"You have surely recognised the uniform of the factory where you were delivering when you were spoken to by police?"

There was merely silence. After a moment Virtue went on, "Ebeling made for the washroom just before you turned through the factory gates, Mr. Ritson. His work bench does not have any outside view. The men's washroom does. As your van entered the gateway, Ebeling left the washroom—surprisingly, as he had made no use of its facilities, and had merely stood gazing out the window.

"He then went straight to the storeroom where the factory security police arrested him. We suggest that your reason for parking was to listen for assurance, on a two-way radio from your office, or perhaps from some other source, that a demonstration by students was proceeding as planned, was growing violent and that roads were becoming blocked and all available police were on duty at the trouble centre. By prearrangement you were, on such assurance, to drive through the factory gates, as a signal to Ebeling. If you turned away, made a delivery elsewhere first, and arrived at the factory much later, Ebeling would have been back at his factory bench, warned by your non-arrival that he was not to go ahead with his attempt at arson, because the demonstration was not, as you hoped, occupying the police, and blocking access roads to the factory."

His voice went on, suggesting, probing, mentioning the Thought Club too, and Lesie and Bratton. Ritson's reply was silence. A silence that continued, along with Ebeling's, to all questions thrown at him.

When the two men had been taken from the room, Virtue said, turning to Jefferson Shields, "So next time we look for another dodge." His voice was tired, bitter. "We haven't finished, you know. Next time it will come from a different set-up. We've ruined one, but it hasn't finished..."

Then he said more lightly, "But it will take planning, and in the meantime we have those two and we'll be probing into their whole lives. Next time it's going to be harder, too, because these two will be brought into court and the whole story brought into the open. There'll have to be a lull. We'll have a breathing space, because the public will remember and the press and the factories." He asked, "And what about you? Have you been to the Thought Club again? Has..."

"Lesie came to see me."

"And...?" his gaze was intent.

"He threatened to sue me for defamation."

Virtue's shout of laughter was genuine amusement, but the other made no attempt to join in. As he walked away he could hear Virtue still laughing. As he went down the corridor he could hear voices from open doorways. He caught the name Ebeling, but already he had forgotten the two men who had decided that silence was their one defence.

CHAPTER THIRTEEN

Shields knew quite well that the girl was bursting to ask outright what Virtue had wanted; why Shields himself had so abruptly left the office and remained away so long. She bustled—that was the only word for it, he decided irritably —in and out, bringing him letters that could have waited, messages that were trivial, cups of coffee that were unasked for and unwanted.

He let her wait. There were other things to think about, statements and fragments of talk, the expression on faces that had looked into his own, to remember and consider, and there were the photos that Michael Morrow, true to his promise, had had sent round.

He took his time over it all, ignoring the girl. Then finally he said, "Sit down," but when she had obeyed he didn't mention Virtue, or the reason for his own leaving of the office. Instead he asked without giving any reason, or lead to the subject, "Did Oliver Harrap go frequently to the Thought Club? Does he know Athol Lesie and Rex Bratton well? Or slightly? Or hardly at all?"

Ann said, "So you know about me and Harry?"

He was remembering that Detrick had called the other man Harry, too, while he waited, without answering, for her to go on.

When she realised that he wasn't going to answer, she said, "Yes, he went quite often. It was, well, central, a place where people, friends, those who were interested in the things he was, could meet and talk."

"Other conscientious objectors?"

"Not only that!" She was frowning, impatient at his lack of understanding. "Everyone talks about *that*. They seem to forget all the other things about Harry. He's mad on skiing, for instance. Whenever he could scrape up enough spare cash he went to the Snowy. He has a keen interest in politics, too—and no, I don't mean the Communist claptrap. If anything, Harry's right on the far side of that sort of thing, but he had ideas and plans—he thought the government was wrong on a whole lot of points."

He smiled at that. "Along with the majority of us? Go on, then."

She relaxed slightly, gave him a half smile back and went on, "And he was deeply interested in crime. Oh, not the reading of detective stories and following crime cases sort of interest, but a wonder about the reasons for men turning to it—that sort of thing. I remember—" She stopped, then went on harshly, "He told me not to worry. He joked about things. Going to prison, you know. He told me that he'd gain a first-hand chance to talk to criminals and get to know them. He made it sound as though it was all going to be part of a study course in something that interested him." She stopped. For a minute she stayed quiet and silent, her eyes closed, then she said, "I seem to have strayed from the subject, but I get furious when Harry's name's mentioned and the first, and last, thing people say about it is, 'Oh, the Conshie', as though there was never anything more to him than that, and never will be.

"The conscientious objector part was only a small thing to him really, but he's stubborn and he has courage, and he said that if everyone went around like sheep, life would be hopeless. So he went to prison because he refused to give in on that point." She shook her head. "He went to the Thought Club because people came there who interested him on other subjects. It's wrong, whatever the police, a lot of other stickybeaks, think. About the Thought Club I mean. Just because they help organise demonstrations and the demonstrations get violent, outsiders talk and hint. It's not fair. Harry," she said it definitely as though the opinion settled the matter for good and all, "Harry said it was quite unfair." She added quickly, "Other people, the demonstrators, and they're the ones who really know, aren't they—they thought it unfair, too."

"Why?"

"I'm not sure really." Hesitant now, she pointed out, "I'm not a University student. I've never followed the demonstrations. Harry wanted me to, sometimes, but I couldn't be earnest that way, or active, either. I guess you could say I'm a bit cowardly," her smile was diffident, "but I shrink from the sort of thing." She looked down at her hands, was silent a long time, then said abruptly, "It seems to me it's wrong. There, that's the honest truth." She looked up at him again. "Just because you've opinions about something doesn't mean you can choke a whole city, make a terrible uproar, disturb everyone else. Why," there was muted laughter in the admission, "why it sounds to me like cats in the night disturbing everyone because that's the way they consider best to make love!

"But get back to what you were asking. Harry used to say that sometimes a whisper would circle about—wasn't it odd that so many demonstrations got violent—but the people who'd helped organise and worked with Lesie and Rex Bratton would shout it down. People liked to hint there was a political bias to the Thought Club, so Harry said, and that was because Bratton was a Communist, but Harry used to laugh at the whole idea.

"He said," she confided, "that Rex Bratton wasn't any more a real dyed-in-the-wool Commie than Harry himself. That it was just a front Bratton put on to attract the Left-wing crowd, so that they'd use the club's organisation too, and the Club wouldn't get landed with the tag of being strictly Far-Right in their views."

She demanded, "Do you think that yourself?"

"I haven't discussed politics with him, or Communism either," Jefferson Shields pointed out. He pressed, "So Harrap always considered the place one of probity, innocence, straightforwardness, honesty?"

She hesitated over that. "I suppose so. Honestly, I was never so interested in the place or the demonstrations either, that I wanted Harry to spend his time talking to me about them." Her eyes smiled behind the black-rimmed glasses, "I wanted him to talk about things that were important to me, to us."

He pressed again, "He never spoke, hinted, of something wrong, criminal..."

"No." She stopped, then began again, "Those last few days before they picked him up and shut him up," she looked sharply away, grimacing slightly, "everything was fearfully disorganised and out of kilter. We all knew they were coming for him, you see. He'd been to court and he'd been given three days to obey the command to report to camp. He wasn't going. His parents were backing him up. Oh yes," she nodded, the blonde hair swinging about her shoulders with the swift movement, "they've been active all along in backing him up, and we all just sat around waiting.

"Harry would start talking about one thing and then forget what he was talking about, so that the subject dwindled away. It was all so—nerve-wracking, you see. He seemed terribly anxious that nobody was going to say he wasn't genuine. He kept saying that people might claim he was just a coward—that it wasn't a matter of conscience at all. Over and over again he'd say things like, 'If there's a hint of that sort of thing they'll never let me out' and again, 'It would rebound on us all—Dad and Mum, too and everyone who's helped.' All that sort of anxiety and the horror of waiting was all mixed up with other things, but I remember he spoke of the Thought Club once. He seemed quite bitter. Oh, not towards those two men. It was along the lines of ... he seemed to think they were fools. Deluded fools. That's what he said, and there was a lot about them just being tools, that they were being used. He added, 'Like we are, the students, the demonstrations, too. We're all being used and we've been fools.'

"No," the denial was sharp. "I don't know what he meant, and it didn't seem important and anyway the talk was ragged, a bit senseless and it dwindled away without him saying anything more.

"It just popped into my head now. I'm afraid it doesn't help. It doesn't mean anything, except ... you see, he obviously didn't think there was anything crooked about them."

"How long ago did he go to prison?" Shields asked.

"Seven weeks and two days ago," the answer came with a depth of feeling that told she'd counted every minute of it.

"A week before Robyn Calder's death? Have you been to see Harrap since?"

"Yes. As soon as they'd let me go. That was a month afterwards. He wasn't allowed visitors at first. They said it was routine, that it gave a man a chance to settle down—things like that. I don't know whether that was truth or just another pinprick to teach him a lesson, but we had to accept it. I went as soon as they'd given me permission."

"He knew about Robyn Calder? What did he say?"

She said flatly, "He was sick. I mean that. Physically sick. He told me it was the worst shock he'd ever had; that it made his whole imprisonment seem pointless, ridiculous. He'd been sent there because he wouldn't take up arms, and then a girl who'd supported him was killed by arms, and that made her death seem ten times worse. That first day—the whole time he could talk of nothing else. He couldn't say a word about himself, or me, or his people, or friends—anything but Robyn. Even now—I saw him at the weekend—" there was a hint of defiance in the admission as though the fact that she was visiting a prison, while acting as his secretary, might prove unpalatable to him, "even now he still talks about it, and he knows now there's going to be trouble. That's another strain for him to carry. He's worried sick about the inquest and the fact that because of him others are going to get into serious trouble.

"The whole thing's impossible!" Suddenly she was weeping wildly, helplessly.

CHAPTER FOURTEEN

That Wednesday was not as brightly sunlit as the previous day. The long rickety staircase with its cracked linoleum and unpleasant walls was dark, and at that time of day, just after noon, the whole building had a curious air of desertion and silence.

Only when Jefferson Shields moved upwards on the last flight of treads did the silence break, the sound of music growing louder and louder, till it beat softly, pleasantly, on his ears, through the closed door to the studio.

This morning Michael Morrow wasn't dressed in a neat dark business suit. A long faded-blue dustcoat covered his clothes. There was a tear in one sleeve, above the elbow, and the collar was rubbed and frayed, but Morrow's smile was as bright as before, his welcome as generous, as he ushered his guest inside.

Suddenly Shields was reminded of another man, only a little bigger than Morrow—a man with the same air of ease and chirpiness.

His gaze, when he had taken the offered chair and was facing the other man, was direct, thoughtful, appraising. He remained silent while Morrow rattled on, the small plump hands gesticulating, moving, darting together and apart. "You getting anywhere? I don't see how you can, and, d'you know something? I'm disappointed, and your eyebrows are going to hit the ceiling," a plump hand gestured towards the open skylight, "or maybe go right through that and fly away, when I say why, because I'm disappointed there wasn't a fire this morning. For why, you're going to ask that. Didn't you know there was a demonstration? There were handbills being handed out last night all over the city, telling everyone interested to attend a big rally against conscription, and that's always good for a real dust-up. The veterans get into the act. 'I served in the war,' he thumped his chest and ranted hoarsely, 'and what was good enough for me is bloody well good enough for the twenty-year-olds today.' I thought there'd be a dust-up, and there'd be a fire, too, only the latter never happened and funnily enough the march fizzled out too, after a brisk bunfight came to nothing.

"Maybe," his gaze was shrewd, watchful and questioning, "Maybe someone's blabbed? I was told last evening to keep my mouth shut, or else. I didn't ask what that meant. Virtue acted like a cat on hot bricks and his answer might've given me palpitations. I've a weak heart."

"I doubt it." At the blank silence, Shields reminded bluntly, "You attend these demonstrations. You face violence. You have been in the thick of fighting—your photos reveal it. No man with a weak heart would dare risk that sort of activity."

Morrow laughed. "That was smart," he congratulated. "But talk of a weak heart gets you out of a whole lot of trouble sometimes, and a whole lot of dirty work."

"Do you dislike dirty work?" Jefferson Shields was spreading the contents of the folder he had brought, out on to the table beside them. He said, "They were not very successful photographs, were they?"

Almost sullenly Morrow shifted so that he could see plainly, as he said, "I told you you'd get nothing helpful, but you asked for the prints and I sent them." His hand roughly shuffled them together. "It was a waste of my time printing them, wasn't it?"

"No. Where are the rest of them?"

There was silence. Then Morrow asked, "Now what do you mean by that?" His tone was quite light.

"Exactly what I said. Where are the rest of them? Where are the good photos—the ones that developed successfully? The ones that reveal faces, the ones..." He said sharply, "Don't be stupid, and obstructive. You're a man who has made a career, and a successful one," his gaze flicked over the comfortable room, "from photography. You're skilled, and you have, so you claim, a hobby-horse. You are very interested in demonstrations. You attend them, not only to get photographs you can sell to the press, but for your own ends.

"No man who is skilled, who is determined to get a worthwhile photo, would invariably finish up with photos that are too blurred for identification of the people in them; which reveal only blacked out sections, backs, blurred profiles . . . where are the others?"

He broke across the slurred beginning of protest with a sharp, "Do you expect me, the police, the public, to believe that in all these months of work only one photograph of hundreds, came out clearly enough to show a demonstrator who was armed—and that demonstrator happened, by an amazing coincidence, to be a girl who was killed?

"You have given yourself away on a dozen points." Now he was impatient, angry at the other's continued silence. "You were forced to take that photograph of Robyn Calder to the police. Other people were in it. They *knew* a photograph had been taken. They had seen the wretched girl, too, and they knew there was a photo. One of those people actually tried to get your camera away from you.

"Of course they were going to read in the press that a girl had died. You yourself have admitted that the evening press that day carried a photograph of Robyn Calder. So those other four in your photograph were going to recognise it, also. If they came forward, if the police rounded them up some other way, and they said, loudly and clearly, 'A photographer took a snap, and she was armed,' the police were going to ask, loudly and clearly also, where was the photograph and where was the photographer.

"It would be one step from that question to them contacting the press and asking what photographer might have been present; another step to your name being mentioned; yet a third to your being asked to attend a line-up at the police station, and a final step to your identification by one of those four, especially the PMG man who chased you.

"You were forced to hand over the print. You could have given no reasonable explanation for withholding it, but

152

you have reasons for withholding those others—the ones that are as good as the ones of Robyn Calder."

"All right, so I had a reason." Michael Morrow shrugged. He said, frankly, "I'm rather hating you, you know." His smile was disarming. "Of course you've guessed the answer, or worked it out. It all boils down to my hobby-horse. Sure, there were other photos. I wasn't going to bring them to light. Where would it lead?" His plump hands spread wide. "To more publicity. I didn't want those demonstrations to get any more than they already had. I found out by myself who was in what photos. Actually there weren't many that turned out well. That one of the girl was a bit of a fluke. The space round the fountain was fairly clear—the centre of the whirlpool sort of effect. It's not often that happens—usually there's too much of a crush round you for you to use a camera at all.

"There were a few that were good. I traced the people in them and I asked a few bright questions on the sly. I told them 'No names, no packdrill, no publicity, so long as you talk to me frankly.'

"Well, I've never raked up a thing." Again came the disarming smile. "It's all been the same, and honestly, Shields, I've never had reason to doubt the stories I got. All of them were the same. All of them said they hadn't gone armed to the demonstrations, but all of a sudden, a hand thrust something into theirs with a 'Take that!' or 'Here, quick!' and it was perfectly natural for their own hand to close over whatever it was. Why should I doubt it's the truth?"

"Where are the photos?"

"Burnt. Believe me?" he challenged.

"Oh yes. I believe you." He added, "Just as I believe your statement that you had no reason to doubt these demonstrators' word. Of course you hadn't. You knew it was the truth."

Quite unemotionally he said, "You are a deplorable creature, Mr. Morrow. There are people who have used those demonstrations for political reasons, just as you have thrust firmly and eagerly under my nose, to draw attention from yourself. I don't pretend to understand the motives be-hind such actions—perhaps the users have other loyalties, are so confused or so tied to other ideologies that they think they are behaving rightly. What I do know is that you have used the demonstrations for the sake of personal gain.

"You know quite well, have always known, that what you were doing was abominable. I do not know who helped you. Someone had to. I do know that you have made many mis-takes. You told me the truth yesterday when you said that the news that I wished to see you gave you what you described as the heebies.

"You panicked badly, but you thought you were making a safe circle round yourself with emphasis on the political angle, on the subject of strikes and fires. You failed to see that for a man whose hobby-horse was the reason for these demonstrations going wrong, you failed lamentably on one question.

"I mentioned the Thought Club. This is the place where demonstrations are organised; where many originate; about whose owners there are whispers and rumours. Yet to my question you dismiss them with the statement you know nothing that isn't common knowledge. If you had been honestly trying to find out why those demonstrations turned to violence you would have been deeply involved with that Club and with the two men who run it. You would have been a constant visitor, probing, questioning, as the police were doing.

"Your brushing aside of my question sounded the alarm to me. The absence of worthwhile photos was the second. The stories I had heard of two people, at least, who had had weapons thrust into their hands was another. Alarm grew when I realised that that was something that could have happened many, many times and always the victim would remain silent, sweating, as one such victim put it to me, for fear he would be found out, for fear someone would point a finger at him and say he had been armed, and he was arrested.

"That same victim spoke of how such victims feel, know-ing that police and photographers are everywhere. Being caught while armed would be certain to lead to police prosecution, to possible expulsion from the University, for a student. For others—and many outsiders are involved in these demonstrations, too—it could involve loss of job, of career prospects, of reputation.

"For some it could be worse. There was a man who was sent to prison as a conscientious objector. He had stood fast on that point. Before he went to prison he spoke bitterly of these demonstrations being used, the demonstrators being tools. His greatest anxiety was that he might have thrown at him a claim that he was not at all genuine—that he was a coward, a shrinker from duty, lurking under the covering of talk of conscience.

"I think, if he is questioned now, and made to speak out, that he might tell a story, Mr. Morrow. He will say, as others did, that in the mêlée of a demonstration, a voice cried, 'Here, quick!', or 'Take that!' and suddenly he found himself armed.

"He, a conscientious objector, remember. What if he was approached and shown a photograph of himself, in a riot, clearly armed? No wonder he was panic stricken those last few days of his freedom. He could see himself and his parents, his supporters and whole cause brought into disrepute.

"He would pay, or his parents would, heavily for the suppression of that photo. So would other parents pay to save their children from prosecution and expulsion. So would others pay to protect their reputation and careers."

Morrow shrugged. The plump hands were quite still in his lap. He said lightly, "That'd be a hard job to prove."

"Perhaps. Since I heard about Oliver Harrap's anxiety, I am not so certain. He is bitterly upset over Robyn Calder's death. If it was put to him that the blame is to be thrust on the girl herself—that it will be made to appear she went deliberately armed, and the arms were used against her, and that she would never have died but for her own actions, I think he will speak out. He's been protecting himself, his cause, everyone who has backed him up in his stand, up to now.

"If he speaks out, I think there's a good chance others will break their silence. You see, Mr. Morrow, up to now they have stood alone. Frightened and alone. They haven't dared discuss what happened to them, for fear the story of the photo comes out and it is thrown at them they had good reason to pay for its burning, because they were wholly guilty of arming themselves. When they know they don't stand alone..." He shook his grey head. He stood up, "I think they will come forward. Slowly, perhaps. One here, and then another, and finally a steady stream, all eager to talk and to nail down the person who has so attacked them."

"I never appeared in person." Morrow was smiling. "All right, so tell me that there had to be a photographer and finally it'll come round to my doorstep. So tell me."

He stared after the thin grey figure moving towards the door. He cried hysterically after it, "So tell me!" and when the grey figure went on moving and the door opened and the tall figure went through, he ran after it. He cried out, down the dark well of staircase after the other man, "Aren't you *afraid* of me? Aren't you afraid of what I might do to you?" And when only silence answered him, he started to run down the stairs. Then he stopped. After a little he turned and went slowly back to the big studio.

Shields heard the door close. The stairway became dark. He had to grope his way down, one hand on the scrawled, filthy walls. He didn't look back.

.   .   .

Virtue was openly smiling, but he warned, "Unless someone is willing to speak, it'll be impossible to prove. He can stand up in any court in the country and claim it's nothing but moonshine and he'll get away with it. It is all supposition, and you know it."

"Yes, but I think Harrap will talk. That's my hope."

Virtue suddenly doubted, "You don't even know for sure that that happened to him. There could be a dozen reasons

156

why those last few days of his freedom he—"

"Perhaps, but look how vulnerable he was. Terribly vulnerable. Just a hint of him having been armed in any demonstration and where was his claim of conscience? Where were his parents and his supporters? Made to look complete fools and dupes, of course. He was so vulnerable no man in Morrow's racket would overlook him.

"It's all very well to claim that in a mêlée of that sort it would be difficult to pick someone out. I doubt very much if that would be so. You would be pressed in alongside other people and however you were swept along by a crowd behind, or beside, or in front of you, you would still be close to the same people.

"Look at those four in the photo of Robyn Calder. They were swallowed up in the crowd, pressed together and tossed out, almost together, and all in the same area. Pressure of the crowd around them kept them together.

"You would need only to mark your quarry and have the photographer to one side; the man who was to hand over the arms on the other, and then herd him, pressing close to him, till suddenly the victim is armed and the man who has armed him has forced his way ruthlessly to one side, creating a small space in so doing, and allowing the photographer to do his work.

"Every one of them will be vulnerable, like Harrap. Whitty —it was tried on him and failed, and there'd always naturally be some failures—is a University student. His people are obviously more than comfortably off. Robyn Calder was the daughter of a parking policeman. He might not have much money, but he has a reputation to watch. Could he have afforded to have it said in public that his daughter was vicious, violent, undisciplined? Could he have faced her appearance in court, charged with being armed with a dangerous weapon and, possibly, inciting a riot?

"You'll find the victims among the ones with the most to lose, the most reasons for keeping quiet for good and all."

"I don't say you wouldn't be right." Virtue sounded abstracted. He said shortly, "We would have caught on to it if we'd known Morrow attended all these riots; if he'd spoken out about his hobby-horse. We'd have wanted to see what photos he'd taken at other times—the whole thing..." He stopped. He apologised, "That sounds ungracious, or worse. I'm only saying ... no leave it. I'm grateful. Come to another point, the man, or the men, who were in this with Morrow? You suspect Lesie and Bratton of course? They organised the damn things, they'd know who was taking part, they could pinpoint a victim..." He gave a jerk of laughter. "And there's more profit than nine hundred and thirty seven dollars in it.

"So it wasn't political at all. Or is it that, too, with them?"

"I doubt it. Morrow was too quick to use that angle. Harrap himself openly laughed at Bratton's talk of being a Communist. He told others it was a pose, a front, a coverage, a drawcard to the Leftist wing of the University and their friends.

"I haven't talked politics to him. I wouldn't know, but as you have pointed out, there is what Lesie calls lovely, lovely money involved in blackmail." There was no humour in the statement, only distaste. He warned, "If someone will only speak out, Morrow is in trouble. He is a photographer. He attended these demonstrations. Where are the *good* photos he should be able to display, but can't. Perhaps you couldn't prove it was he ... but suspicion will ruin him and he knows it. The Club is different. They can slide away from trouble. It will be the old story-line— they merely organised the demonstrations and they cannot be held responsible for what outsiders do. They have only to throw up their hands in respectable horror at the talk of this racket and..." He shrugged.

He asked, "You've investigated them from all angles, I am sure. Their bank accounts?"

"Nothing. Scale of living is consistent with club profits. Bratton is actually married. A child, too. All quite respectable. They'd keep it like that, of course, knowing we were on their backs, till they were ready to cash in and skip. No, I agree, it's not likely we'll ever be able to pull them in, if they *were* Morrow's little helpers.

"This angle..." he hesitated, "about the dead girl—the ball you tossed to Lesie and Bratton about maybe she learned something she shouldn't have, and she was killed for it. Is it worthwhile playing it up, do you think? Tossing it back at them as fast as they try tossing it out of their backyard? They might be panicked into trying to run and we'd get on to whatever cash they've hidden away, if so. They'd have to try to account for that."

Shields shook his head. "They've stayed put," he reminded, "under all these months of your continued probing and questioning; under having the police arrive at their premises brazenly or secretly."

There was silence between them, until Shields asked, "Could you arrange for me to see Oliver Harrap?" At the other's quick upward glance he added, "Before anyone else questions him? There is the fact he is deeply distressed over Robyn Calder's death. I would like to add to that distress, probing at him, and *then* talk of blackmail. If he is sufficiently softened, sufficiently reminded of her death and the causes for it, I think he may well speak out. I would like to discuss the Thought Club with him, too, and this man who entered Robyn Calder's life. That question irritates me.

"It is quite possible that in something he mentions of his visits to the Thought Club there will be some angle of use to you. It's doubtful, or possible. As you might say yourself, we can hope for the best, while expecting the worst.

"There is another point. If Harrap was attacked, made a victim of Morrow's racket, as I firmly believe is the case, it was in the last days of his freedom. He had no time, whatever his feelings, to try and discover who had placed him in that impossible position. His father would have had to have been the one to pay off Morrow, however, and he had his freedom.

"Oh yes, there must have been attempts somewhere, on the part of someone, to track down who was responsible, and it came to nothing, but Harrap remains in a position of vulnerability.

"Take a look at the ordinary person. If blackmail was

paid, almost certainly that person would never again be rash enough to place themselves in such a position. They would be most unlikely ever again to attend a demonstration. In the case of a student they would owe it to their parents to never again cause them a great loss of money. If, at any time in the future, it was stated those photos, or copies of them, were still in existence, they could claim they had never again, from that point onwards, be involved in anything approaching violence.

"The law, public opinion, their employers, the University, would take a very lenient attitude then. It is one thing to be discovered armed in a riot. It is another for the person to stand up in court and claim that he or she has never again, since that day, had anything to do with either violence or demonstrations—that they have reformed.

"Harrap's case is entirely different. He is in prison, and at any time another copy of that photo could be brought to light, another demand made for payment to destroy it. For so long as he persists in his arguments; for so long as his case has prominence, and right into the future for that matter, the public would treat the appearance of a photo of him armed, in the middle of a riot, with outraged fury. The whole cause he has espoused so drastically would become the focus of jeers and contempt. He has a tremendous amount to lose and so have his parents and his supporters.

"Harrap can't be unintelligent. He is supposed to be brilliant, in point of fact. He can't have failed to realise he remains vulnerable. In prison he would have time to think and to plan, and by now he must have realised on all his memories and knowledge of the demonstrations and their organising and handed the facts to his people.

"There is another point," he reminded. "How did the money come to be paid? It will have been done some way to give Morrow and his co-workers protection, but even the best of such protection has collapsed before this.

"Harrap is the one victim I can be reasonably sure *was* a victim. Possibly your only hope of bringing the case to court. You know yourself how it is—one victim waits for another to speak out first, so that he won't stand out alone. A lot will remain grimly silent of course, and refuse any involvement at all."

Virtue seemed to be looking past him, as though his thoughts had travelled beyond Harrap and beyond Lesie and Bratton and Michael Morrow too, but he said, "I'll make arrangements for you to see Harrap as quickly as possible."

He volunteered, "We've had nothing out of those two we brought in this morning. We've picked up Ritson's wife as well. She works in the bakery. The manager—one of the family who own the whole concern—gives a simple reason for the two-way radios in the vans. They supply shops, canteens, all over the city. They can pick up unwanted stock, shunt it elsewhere, make emergency deliveries, save unnecessary trips back and forth to the bakery through heavy traffic. All quite straightforward, on the surface. The family have had the business for over forty years." He admitted wearily, "And it doesn't take four years even to turn a man, or his whole family, into a bad 'un, a traitor, a criminal, and yet . . . the factory's had contracts for supplying canteens at every factory that's been hit by a fire. Oh yes, they supply dozens more, too, and yet . . ."

"Mrs. Ritson has worked there for three years. She runs the radio control. She'd be older than Ritson I'd say, with the appearance of a middle-aged woman with no interests except home and job and husband. She says we're crazy." He eased himself in his chair. "She doesn't say anything else. She just laughs and says there's no use trying to answer questions, because we're crazy." He asked sharply, suddenly smiling, mocking a little with the question, "Are you going to send in a bill now to Detrick—you've done what he asked."

There was reproof in the quiet, "I can give him an answer. I still haven't proof. Not until I've talked to Harrap and perhaps not even then," and a demand in the sharper, "Could you phone the prison—now?"

CHAPTER FIFTEEN

Shields was reminded how easily one could draw a wrong conclusion; how easily be led astray, because all he had been told of Oliver Harrap had conjured up a mental picture of a tall, thin figure, pale-faced, withdrawn in manner because of the beliefs that had made him an outcast.

Oliver Harrap was a mockery of such imaginings. He was big, with a maturity both of body and expression that would have made Detrick appear beside him as callow; Whitty as a child; Lesie and even Rex Bratton as a pale shadow of what they purported to be.

He thought how well the tall, straight, strong figure would have looked beside Chris Stowe, and wondered why he had thought of that. Chris has chosen her own man, he reminded himself. This man, with the close-cropped dark hair and the grey-green eyes, and wide mouth with an upward tilt to the corners, was Ann Aveyard's ... perhaps, if all went well, Shields reminded himself, again. Partings, and disgrace and imprisonment had made lovers galore drift away and Ann was being pressured by her family.

He pushed the thought to one side, as Harrap's brief hesitation in the doorway of the cream-walled, barred-windowed room, ended, and he came forward with firm steady stride, the green-grey gaze fixed on his visitor, curious, enquiring, interested.

The statement held an undercurrent of laughter as he said, "I was asked if I wanted to see a visitor. Now what would you, and they ...", a little jerk of his dark head went to the door closing behind him, "have said if I'd refused? Because I don't know you, or your name. By the way it was spoken it was evident I should have known it."

The dark brows rose in question as he sat down in the hard wooden chair opposite the older man.

Jefferson Shields answered only, "Nigel Detrick, along with others—with Ann Aveyard..." he paused, seeing a quick flicker across the strong young face, and then the closing down on all expression, "employed me—to find out who was at the back of this rioting, this destruction of demonstrations that should have been peaceful."

The studied indifference was instantly gone. The question came jerkily, "What've you found out then? Or have you just started?" There was disapointment in the latter thought, in the sharp, "And just who are you?"

"I deal in puzzles and problems. Leave that question aside. My name means nothing to you. Ann Aveyard however, recognised it as the name of a possible help for Detrick, for others at the University. You know of course that there is serious trouble over the death of Robyn Calder?"

For an instant the heavy lids shuttered down over the grey-green eyes, then Harrap was gazing full at him. He said, "I know," and added, "The inquest is next week."

"Detrick fears he, possibly others, will face University expulsion," Jefferson Shields finished for him. "Take, firstly, the subject of Robyn Calder."

Again the eyes closed. The deep voice said clearly and definitely, "I'd prefer not to," and then his gaze was open again and he brushed that aside with, "No, forget that. You want to talk about it. Go on from there."

"You are deeply distressed over her death." It was a statement not a question, but the other broke in sharply.

"All the winds of the world couldn't wail what I feel ... I'm sorry." He grinned. "That sounds purely fanciful, doesn't it? Take it, I was badly cut-up. It was dreadful, abominable —all the words that follow on from there. I didn't know her well, but I'm responsible for her death. That makes it even worse, to me. When I heard I nearly went to the governor here. I nearly said, 'Look, all I've stood for, and stood against, is a mockery now. I came here as a symbol for non-violence and the meeting in support of me turned so violent that a girl is dead.'

"Perhaps that sounds as though I was only considering it from one point of view—my own. That's not so, but it was so shocking ... frightening, too. There were all those people—all of them against violence, and then suddenly ... everything was so violent that a girl died. Where's the sense in it?"

He shook his head. "I'm sorry. I've been babbling. I'm not used to the silence in here," he apologised with another grin. "I was always talking, non-stop my family claimed, before I came here. I've a cell to myself. That's a privilege from what I can make out." He laughed openly. "It's supposed to save me from contamination from the others in here, but the nights're so long. You get locked up so early." There was no self-pity, only a statement of fact. "It's good for studying though."

He stopped, "Look, I'm babbling again. Let's get to the point. You wanted to take the subject of Robyn Calder. All right then, take it. *You* talk for a change."

"You said you didn't know her well?"

"That's so."

"How well?"

"Oh ... well, we met around the University. At debates, and that sort of thing. Not at lectures."

"Did you ever visit her home? Invite her to a party at your own, with friends of her own choosing?"

"No, nothing at all of that sort. We didn't meet on those terms."

"So you are not an authority on her home background, her close friends, any man she might have known?"

The dark head was shaken. "Not a thing, except ... I did meet her father once." He grinned. "Neither of us got anything out of the meeting to want us to follow it up. He came to the University Open Day—you know the sort of thing—all the maiden aunts and giggling young sisters and parents and grandparents shuffling around wide-eyed, with the students trying to dodge the tutors and the tutors trying to dodge everyone?

"When I bumped into Robyn the old chap was towing her around, making her point out the buildings to him. She introduced us. Unfortunate. I was wearing an anti-conscript button, and he looked at it, pop-eyed. He said, in a tone that put me down with the eternally damned, 'So you're a pacifist,' and threw at me, 'I call that another word for shirker,' in a tone that said his was the only opinion that counted. The look he tossed at Robyn said that he expected her to take heed and meekly agree.

"I was amazed when I heard she'd joined that march, the demonstration in my support. She never seemed the type to me who'd buck her father, and it looked to me, that day, as though he dominated, bossed her. She must have had more character, been less bossed about..."

"Have you considered that she might have become involved with a man who was, like yourself, a conscientious objector?" Shields suggested.

The grey-green eyes opened wide. He said slowly, "It's odd, but I hadn't. It's quite possible." He admitted frankly, "I'd like to think it was not only possible, but definitely true, because then it wouldn't ... the blame I mean, seem so much to belong to me. It wouldn't be me myself who'd drawn her into..." he seemed to be speaking almost to himself and the older man broke across the words.

He asked, "Did you know that she was so frightened at one demonstration that she ran away and tried to find shelter in nearby buildings?"

"Yes. That's not uncommon you know. It's a darn sight harder than you can believe, if you're an outsider, to keep your head when you find yourself in the middle of a fighting, yelling mob."

"So that if you were frightened and someone thrust an iron bar into your hand you might lose your head sufficiently to hold on to it?"

Harrap was no longer looking at him. At anything except the far wall. He said without expression, "I expect not."

Shields said softly, "Robyn Calder was armed."

He saw the wave of shock start at the wide mouth, tremble it and part the lips, then ripple across the cheekbones, and widen the eyes to startled awareness.

He went on crisply, "She was photographed."

The demand came sharply. "How do you know?"

"The photograph was handed to the police." Harrap frowned at that and his visitor added pointedly, "It was a matter of necessity, or perhaps her father could have been made to pay well for its suppression."

This time the effect of the shock wasn't so noticeable, as though the boy had been half prepared for it. He sat slackly, waiting silently until the other man went on, "Four people were in the photo besides the girl. One tried to assault the photographer. Any, or all, of them were likely to come forward, or be found by the police. The photograph had to be produced as a purely fortuitous piece of photography, before mention of a photograph was made and enquiries begun as to why the photographer had not come forward.

"It was different in your own case," he challenged bluntly. "You were alive. You, of all people, could never have a photograph produced showing you armed, in the middle of a riot. How were you contacted? How was the demand made for blackmail?" He thrust at the still, white-faced figure, with the added, "The police are certainly going to mention this at the inquest. There is one boy at least—Graham Whitty—you probably know the name?—who will be forced to admit that in the mêlée of another riot a weapon was thrust into his hand. Nothing happened to him however. The photograph, if one was taken there, was apparently no good.

"He was lucky. You were not. Listen to me carefully before you think only of yourself, your parents, the cause that's brought you here to prison. There are going to be suggestions, Whitty is going to give evidence on the witness stand; there are going to be rumours and hints. It is inevitable that a few people, at the very least, will think of you as a possible victim.

"Oh yes, once the matter is out in the open the racket will die a natural death. You might think only of that point and brush all the others aside. I don't intend to let you. You are the only one we are fairly sure was a victim. The police want proof of it. I want the questions I put to you answered. For a start—how were you contacted? We'll take it for granted that a weapon was thrust into your hand one day, and that a photograph was taken."

Oliver Harrap said harshly, "Stop there. Right there. No, it's no use trying to beat me down with words. A lot of people have tried doing that about other things. Stop, while I think it out."

He remained silent for so long that the older man was growing definitely uneasy. He knew that the first shock, the first panic, had died, and he had counted on that helping to thrust resistance aside.

Then Harrap said, low-voiced, "It was just after the first court case. Before my appeal was dismissed. There was a demonstration about the ballot system for conscripting national servicemen. It was an outsider who began the violence. He threw a half brick into the middle of the crowd, along with a few words of obscenity. Someone grabbed him, and threw *him*. Next thing everyone seemed to be fighting. I don't consider," his expression was reflective, remembering, "that the police were a bit of help. They added to it, unintentionally. Just their appearance, their demand for everyone to move on and break things up, made people start arguing with them and brought further anger on both sides.

"That's beside the point, of course. Someone banged against my side and a voice yelled at me, 'Take it quick!' and ... well, I took whatever it was. I didn't stop to think, you understand? I honestly didn't realise that a photograph had been taken, because as soon as I saw what it was I tried to press through the crowd, to find who'd handed it to me.

"I didn't get anywhere. I tossed the thing—it was an ugly looking home-made cosh—as far past the crowd as I could. I didn't want anyone to use it, but I was terrified of being caught with it.

"Next evening there was a phone call. To my father. It was quite simple. A photograph had been taken of me, very obviously armed, in the middle of a riot. I would find a copy of it in the letterbox outside, at that moment.

167

"No," he looked up for the first time, directly at the older man, "there was no one about. Just the photo in a sealed envelope, it was a shocker," he admitted frankly, "and it would have finished me. We talked it over. We knew quite well that that was only the start, but there was nothing we could think of to do, except pay up."

"How much was the demand?"

Harrap grimaced. "One thousand dollars. That was ridiculous, of course, when they could have asked much fatter greasing of their hands, considering my position right then. It was another pointer to it being the first bite. There's been another since," he admitted simply. Then he added, "And no, we didn't consider contacting the police. Would you have done, in our place? The police have little sympathy for a Conshie for a start, and whatever they did that photo would get publicity, and it was only my word that I hadn't deliberately armed myself. Do you understand that point? Because that's the main thing to remember. Everyone would have said I'd armed myself.

"My parents hoped they'd find out something. They didn't."

"How did you pay the money?"

"It was to be paid, in cash—we were told a cheque would do if we liked, but that in that case we wouldn't get the negative until the cheque had been cleared—into a City bank, to the credit of a John Fisher.

"My parents did what they could. They bribed a clerk," he suddenly grinned in real humour, "the bank would have a fit and I bet they'd deny heatedly it could happen, but in every job there's someone who'll take a bribe and you know it—as to what he could tell about John Fisher and his account. That was nothing. John Fisher had an address, which proved a dud. He didn't require statements sent to him. Naturally enough as he didn't live at the address he claimed! He had started the account with a small cash deposit. Only two payments had been added—ours. There were no withdrawals at all. No one in the bank could even remember what he looked like. It's too simple now to open an account. You don't need references, to see the manager, anything at all, except sign your name to bits of paper and hand over some cash."

His voice scorned, "They make it too easy for crooks to operate. I wasn't the only one to be treated that way. I was sure of that, and you've said now that I'm right. Where's the rest of the money been sent? To little accounts all over the country, to a dozen different names like John Fisher. Wouldn't that be so? It's clever, isn't it?" he finished wearily.

"Yes." Shields was frowning. He felt very tired and very depressed. He went on, "The money could be left for months, even longer. Even then he needn't appear to collect it. The account could be transferred, at the signing of a few more papers, to somewhere else in the country. It could be transferred again and again, if the need arose. There would be the risk someone might jib, might pay and be outwardly meek, but go to the police. There was still safety. The police could watch the account, the bank could, and still John Fisher, whatever name he liked to use, would never appear."

He nodded. He said shortly, "I think all those small accounts will have been left deliberately fallow. No one whom we think is concerned has shown signs of having money he hasn't properly accounted for. They've been waiting. The money was quite safe in the bank. There was no hint that it belonged to them. Then they could swoop in one action, gather it all in and disappear—and at any bank, if there was the slightest delay in immediate pay-out, they would take alarm and run from that account. Why not? There were all the rest waiting for them to collect.

"Yes, it's quite clever." He asked sharply, "Isn't there anything else you can tell me?"

"I'm sorry." Harrap added after a moment, "Now you'll have me brought to court. It will all come out. A lot of people will go on for ever to claim I've lied. You know it." His expression was bleak. "I'm trying to think clearly and it's unpleasant, but ... they ... well, someone who came to see me has hinted I might be out again soon. What happens now if that's so? I'm let free and there's a

169

public row. They'll say my freedom was for services rendered. That all my story in court was a downright lie dreamed up by the students, to get the blame off their shoulders; dreamed up by the University so they could turn a blind eye; dreamed up by the police even ... because old Calder is a parking cop for a start, and he wouldn't want his daughter dubbed as a trouble-maker.

"You've made me put my head on the block, and you know it." There was no anger in the statement, only a grim acceptance. He shook his head violently. "And it's useless saying Graham Whitty can back me up, and that others will come forward to back me, too. What have you got as proof I'm speaking the truth? Just a bank account in the name of a mythical John Fisher. You know what everyone will say to that—that the students, my parents, the University, old Calder himself, opened that themselves to back up this yarn."

He stood up. He said heavily, "I've helped you. Now help me. You've got to find other proof. Fast." A faint smile touched his mouth. "Or my head goes on the block. Remember that and play as fair by me as I've played by you."

.   .   .

Virtue admitted, "The boy's quite right, you know. No one's going to be prepared to believe in it. I could see that all along. His head's going on the block all right. It's a wonder you got him to talk at all."

"Robyn Calder was responsible," Shields explained. "He felt the way Whitty did—responsible. In Harrap's case, doubly responsible. All these six weeks since she died he's been dogged by the knowledge that she died in a demonstration supplying support to himself. That's goaded him unendurably. Now he is faced with the added responsibility that he failed to speak out about the way the students were being armed, so she became a victim in turn and she died."

"If he wants to torture himself..." The words began impatiently and trailed off into silence. The Inspector asked at last, "Do you plump for those accounts not being touched, or for them having been quietly closing all through today? The money would have to go somewhere. If you're Lesie or Bratton you wouldn't dare bring it close to yourself. Safest to leave it lie, do you think? And yet ... they must realise that someone might come forward, and then someone else, and the names and the banks will burst out into the open and they'll lose the money."

"Some of it. Some of the victims would stand on the sidelines to eternity rather than be involved."

There was a long silence the other end of the phone, then Virtue said impatiently, "If they sit pat we're virtually helpless. How can you check every account in every bank in every city and town in the nation?"

"The banks themselves can check on wrong, or fictional addresses," Shields pointed out.

"Even so, where are we? Put a watch on the account, certainly, but they might think freedom is the one thing they're interested in. They might scrap the whole gain. It's been known to happen, you know, and there's no sign of a pro. in this racket, so far as we know. And if the accounts are quietly cleared it could be done without anyone taking an interest. They'd leave a few dollars in each account to keep it running. Otherwise the manager would come out, wanting to have an explanation for a lost account to send to his head office. But if it's kept running ... and they wouldn't take the slightest risk they could be later recognised in their true identities, so where ..."

"Signatures," Shields suggested.

"Oh that, certainly, but do you reckon that Morrow, or Lesie or Bratton would have signed for these accounts. I couldn't credit it. They've been too careful on other points. There has to be someone else. Lesie and Bratton have always been too sure of themselves. You've said that yourself," he reminded. "They must have known that if the racket did break wide open they'd come under instant suspicion. If you look at it that way you'll see there just has to be a fourth man. Someone we don't know about, whose signature is on all those accounts. How do we find *him*?

He'll be closing the accounts and whisking the money out of sight and sitting it out, and what can we do? Nothing. Well?" he demanded impatiently, breaking the silence.

"Yes, there's a fourth man," Shields admitted.

"You don't sound depressed. Or even very interested." There was impatience and anger in the soft voice across the line. He added, as though in excuse of it, "We're picking up one person after another connected with Ritson and Ebeling and the pie factory and I haven't enough words out of any of them to make a one page report." He demanded, "What do you mean to do next?"

"See the four people in that photo."

"What are you after there? I'll warn you frankly I had them squeezed drier than The Inland." There was a faint jeer in his, "Do you expect them to come out and say that after all they saw the man who armed that girl? Our fourth man in the racket?"

"Yes," Shields said definitely and across the startled, yelled, "What?" across the line, he began to speak again.

CHAPTER SIXTEEN

Kate Hough seemed to think he was wasting her time. He took her from cooking the family dinner. She told him so, rubbing the print cotton of her apron nervously between her plump hands, as she faced him in the late afternoon sunshine threading over the furniture in her tiny sitting room.

She said, gaze cocked towards the clock on the wall, "Greta'll be home soon and it's business college night. That means early eating for us all." She added sharply, her round homely face creased in a frown, "It's not fair of you people harassing me the way you're doing. If I'd thought I'd get into all this trouble, going to you, I'd never, never have gone."

"Why *did* you go to the police?" he asked softly.

Her mouth opened, then closed, without uttering a sound. She stared at him silently. "I dunno what you mean by that—but it doesn't sound right to me. Sort of suspicious." The round face was reddening. She said again, "I don't like it. I went because I could see that girl in front of me all the time, mouthing that way that she wanted to get out. It was quite, quite plain," she assured him. Her anger was growing. She thrust at him, "That's why I went. She was scared silly. Just a silly little girl who'd been caught up in something that was too big for her. It was terrible she died, when all she wanted was to get out of that horrible crowd. I thought of that and I thought maybe I can help, so I ..."

"Why? Why think you could help? You gave no information that was worthwhile, about her death."

Her mouth opened that same way and closed after a minute without speaking a word. She said at last, "No, I didn't, because I never saw her die, see, but I thought ...

well, there were a couple of us, four I mean, and that man with the camera, too. I thought, well she shouldn't have died because she was just a silly little girl, that was all, and I thought, maybe some of those others know more than me, only they won't come forward, because there wasn't any photo of her taken in that crowd, in any of the papers. I went through them all carefully. I said to myself, Well, where's the photo? And I thought, maybe that man and the others won't come forward. It's not nice being involved." Her face reddened again, "And look at the trouble it brought on me! So I went to the police and said there was a photo taken. Did they know that? And they said yes, and they said I mustn't talk about her being armed like that, and they showed me the photo.

"It was terribly clear. I looked real silly, too. All of us did. Funnily enough, when I got a look at it, I realised I knew one of the others. Not well—just through us being insured with his firm, you see." She added defiantly, "I wouldn't have given his name to them if I'd realised what it was going to be like. He's probably real mad at me. I did ring him up and say I was sorry about it. He said that well, I'd know better next time wouldn't I, what the police did to you when they got hold of you for something. He's right.

"I could have saved myself the trouble, and the worry, of going really. They'd seen the photo and they talked to us all and none of us knew anything. It was a waste of time," pointedly she glanced at the clock again.

He told her quite definitely, "No, it wasn't a waste of time at all."

．　　　．　　　．

Patrick Frawley was in his pyjamas. He apologised for that, and for his bare feet, as he pattered back through the tiny apartment in a corner of the building that sprawled in ugliness over a tiny suburban plot.

He said over his shoulder, plumping cushions in the disordered living room, "I've had a rotten day. One of those days when every last thing goes wrong. You sell a policy and five months later the place burns down and everyone in the office looks at you as though you ought to be hung, drawn and quartered.

"You're never right in this game. The clients hate you because they don't get as much as they imagined they'd collar if they hit trouble; and head office hates you for selling the policy in the first place instead of one that goes on for fifty years without a claim. You just never win in my game."

He flung himself into one chair, gestured his visitor to another.

Shields asked, "How many games have you, Mr. Frawley? Besides selling insurance?"

Frawley stared at him, then jerked into laughter. "You think I moonlight? Believe me, one job's enough. Come evening and I'm dead on my feet usually. Oh, insurance pays well enough you know—I'm not beefing about that side of it. Anyway, the company frowns on its salesmen taking on any sidelines. Two jobs and you give the impression your company's doing so little business you can't earn a decent living at it."

"What would they think of the sideline of blackmail?" Shields asked.

For only the briefest moment was there silence, then Frawley's eyes opened wide. He asked, "Now what on earth do you mean by that?"

Jefferson Shields sighed. His gaze was on the clock on the disordered corner table. He said crisply, "You're tired, Mr. Frawley. So am I. We'll dispense with preambles, and wasted words.

"You have been associated with Michael Morrow in an abominable racket that has preyed on credulous students, on their parents, on earnest and innocent people. Your name would never have been mentioned in connection with him, with this business, but unfortunately you were recognised, though in the guise of an innocent insurance salesman.

"All along, while considering this racket of having the demonstrators armed ... Don't open your eyes in pretended surprise and innocence," he added in sudden blistering anger, "you know quite well what I am discussing. To return, all the time I have reflected on it and the photographs, I have realised that the whole thing had to happen in a matter of seconds. The victim was armed, the photograph had to be taken at once, or the crowd would part photographer and victim, or the weapon would be discarded.

"That presupposed that the person who armed the victim was almost certainly caught in the lens of the camera in many of the photos. Naturally his face would be deliberately covered, concealed, before the photos were printed, except in one. In that he had to appear. That one was the one taken of Robyn Calder.

"It was inevitable that should be so. The girl was armed. At any second she might drop the weapon, or disappear from sight, so the photograph had to be taken at once, and surprisingly, that space round the fountain was at that moment comparatively clear, so that four people, besides the girl, were clearly visible.

"What was Morrow to do? He had to bring the photograph to light. Actually one of the people concerned—the woman who knew you, Mr. Frawley, had gone to the police and said there was a photo. There was no chance of concealing you. The photograph had to be clear and undamaged. There was no possibility of saying, 'Oh, that photo was no good, it was blurred, out of focus.' The police would still have demanded the negative—the reason why you had destroyed it, if you had done so, when you knew quite well a girl had died in that riot. However one looked at it, Morrow would be in trouble, unless he produced the photograph as it was.

"It seemed safe to do so; when the police contacted you, it seemed safe, also, for you to admit you were the fourth person in the photograph. *Your* refusal to come forward was readily explainable. You had no evidence, unlike Morrow. You were an innocent bystander and such do not like being involved in police inquiries. Your company might not like you being involved, either. Oh yes, it was readily explainable.

"Once found you merely gave the story of an innocent

bystander, caught up in the crowd, pressed into it, spewed out near the fountain, photographed so that you tried to hide yourself from further publicity, and then you were caught up again and spewed out once more.

"It was a perfectly credible story, because it happened to others. But the others carried nothing that could have concealed a weapon, and you did—a briefcase. Certainly Mrs. Hough carried a purse, but it was a tiny thing. It is clearly visible in the photograph. So is your briefcase.

"All along it has seemed to me there were two essentials to the person who was Morrow's partner. He had to have a respectable job, as a cover, so that if he was ever caught up by the police he was an innocent bystander, apologised to, and sent about his real business and never so much as mentioned or brought into court—so that victims from past demonstrations might recognise him.

"That was an important point. I ruled out a student. I ruled out several people mentioned. I wanted a man with a respectable cover as an innocent bystander, a man who could move about the city as he pleased, who was boss of his own time and movements, and who could carry a concealed weapon.

"You had only to be near Morrow, and the two of you performed as a team. You circled your victim, pressed in on him or her on either side, the weapon was transferred from hand to hand and the photo taken, while you forced your way out of the crowd and went on your way—the innocent insurance agent."

Frawley started to laugh. He said lightly, "Honestly, I don't know what all those dramatics mean, but an innocent insurance agent is all I am. As to blackmail..." his arms spread wide, "look at my scale of living. You can have a look at my bank account if you like."

"I am quite certain your coverage is excellent on all points. There remains your handwriting. When finally all the accounts that have been opened for the purposes of blackmail have been found—not so difficult as you perhaps imagine it will be—the signatures on deposit forms and the notation of addresses on bank records will be available for comparison with your own handwriting. You might have been very careful—you most certainly have been—but you never expected to be picked up, no matter what happened to Morrow, or anyone else. I think the handwriting experts will have plenty to work on and convict you."

He added quite mildly, "And I wouldn't try to run away, Mr. Frawley, because there are policemen waiting for you in the corridor outside."

CHAPTER SEVENTEEN

The two men dined early the next evening in a dimly-lit corner of Shields' club. They had spoken very little, and both had been thinking of all that had taken place since Frawley's arrest. He and Morrow had refused all statements and while, all over the city, banks were quietly checking on clients' addresses and accounts, Athol Lesie and Rex Bratton had come smilingly, mockingly, through long questioning that they had parried with one single parrot-cry of "Nonsense!"

From the circle that held Ebeling and Ritson and his wife, the police were moving out in widening rings of enquiry, unhurrying, not depressed by each failure and each silence, because they were confident of final success.

Only when the last sip of coffee had been drained did Virtue break the silence to say, "I've spent too much time on the fire and strike angle. Not enough on other things." Then he laughed ruefully, admitting, "Excuses, excuses! And I admit I took Frawley at his face value and Morrow, too. Perhaps actually I wanted to. Not having to look too hard in their direction left me time to think about other points of the demonstrations."

He added after a moment, "I don't think we'll ever embroil Lesie and Bratton. Oh, there'll be suspicion and distrust. We'll play it up for all we're worth. They'll be forced to shut up shop. That's one satisfaction and now we have Frawley there's no way they can reach those accounts." He laughed in real enjoyment. "You know, there's great satisfaction in that thought, for me. I bet the victims get a kick out of it, too, when the facts come out. There's money all over the country probably that they want and have worked for and need right now, but they were too clever. They kept themselves right out of it and now the only man who can withdraw those accounts is under our gaze."

There was another long silence. Then he said heavily at last, "So you have an appointment with Detrick tonight? And the two girls? Harrap's head will remain on his shoulders; Detrick's on his, too, apparently. What are you going to tell them?"

Shields lifted his gaze. It wasn't really seeing the other man. He said, "Nothing but the truth—that they've been used in many ways, for too many rackets." He glanced at his watch. He apologised, "I'll have to go." Halfway to his feet he asked, "Have you filled that first page of report yet?"

"No." Dead silence. "I'm not depressed. We'll go on reaching out in wider and wider circles till we touch someone who'll talk—for money, for freedom, or just out of sheer funk. There's always someone who proves bribable, some way, in every racket." He congratulated, "We've done very well, and I mean *you* and I."

"Oh yes, very well indeed," Shields admitted, but there was no pleasure in the admission.

. . .

There was no pleasure, either, in his expression as he faced the three hopeful faces, in his office. The overhead lights he had deliberately left out. The faces were blurred, shadowed, outside the pool of light cast from the single lamp on his desk, because he hadn't wanted to see their expressions while he spoke.

He began, "I have done what you asked—or rather, demanded, that I should do. Whether you are satisfied or not must be your own decision, because you have all been used and your motives abused and your whole way of life and your consciences and your causes brought into disrepute.

"Firstly, you have been used to hide a festering sore of disruption to the whole nation. Athol Lesie and Rex Bratton were quite correct, I am now certain, in stating that outsiders were nearly always to blame for inciting these riots. They were begun for the purposes of blocking streets, drawing police away from other areas, making so much publicity for themselves that other news faded into the background. Lesie and Bratton, I am also certain, were well aware of the reasons for the incitement, but they did nothing about it because it served their own ends, and they deliberately added to the rioting for their own purposes."

None of them attempted to interrupt while he went on speaking. Only at one point did Ann Aveyard give a gasp, an hysterical giggle, a stuttered, "Meat pies! Meat pies of all things!" and then she was still again, and the little pool of light from the desk lamp shone on her hand, held firmly in Detrick's.

"That was the first point," Shields concluded. He waited, and was glad of the silence, the non-appearance of questions. He went on, "Secondly, you were used for purposes of blackmail, and that fact will be brought out at the inquest on Robyn Calder, so that blame and interest will shift from ..." he looked at Detrick's shadowed features, "*your* shoulders."

He had never had so attentive an audience as the three who listened to his talk of photographs and a man in pyjamas and bare feet who had laughed and spoken of innocence.

"I have an unpleasant awareness that a few of the more sensational journals have used you and these demonstrations, too. Small incidents have been added to, even fabricated, possibly, in a tirade of hysteria that is merely a mass of words designed to increase the sales of those same wretched papers. Unfortunately a great mass of ordinary people notice only the words and not the hysteria that has been deliberately drummed up to make mountains from molehills, so they keep on purchasing, and more hysteria goes into print to keep them satisfied. A vicious circle that has no ending.

"Leave that point. Take another. You have been used as a cover for crime. Not big crime, not vicious and violent crime—yet, but the demonstrations have become an attraction for car thieves, who can work unhampered because everyone's attention is centred elsewhere; because the police are being taken from their real work to control those demonstrations. A car here, and a car there, vanished in a few minutes, is so part of ordinary city life, that few people think about it, except the victims. Only rarely does insurance cover the full loss, and the inconvenience can be immeasurable. Add the number of vanished cars, one to another, since these demonstrations took precedence over all other events and the total is dismaying.

"You have become a cover, an inducement, also, for the petty thief—the man or woman who will steal from co-workers, or workers in adjoining offices. The police call this petty crime, yet in the past thirteen months a total of over five thousand dollars has vanished from office buildings near the centre of demonstrations. Certainly that would not be the full total." He reminded them, "People faced with the prospect of calling the police, an investigation, a possible arrest and trial, shrink from the whole idea. If the money stolen was small, if it didn't cause real hardship to the victim, it is very possible they would remain silent, but none of the police lists showing the amounts stolen and from where and from whom, list the effects on the victims, and the hardships and the worry.

"In one office alone, in the late afternoon, eight women and girls had just been paid. A demonstration began outside. They were alarmed, fearing they might not be able to leave the building for hours. They all ran from the office—very foolishly, no one can deny—to the other side of the building, to look out and see what was happening. From their purses a total of three hundred and forty dollars vanished, along with a diamond engagement ring one girl had just taken from her finger, before moving towards the washroom.

"It is easy to say that they put temptation in the way of the petty thief. It is just as easy to say that demonstrations encourage the petty thief to watch for an opportunity to carry out his unpleasant work."

He told them, "Leave that point. Take something more. You and these demonstrations had been used again—as a cover for murder."

Their stillness was broken, and their silence. Questions babbled at him, tore at the quietness of the room, wailed in fright and panic from the shadowed faces. He said impatiently, "You came to me with a tale of murder by demonstration, to capture my interest and my help. You never believed in the idea yourselves, but you were right. Robyn Calder was murdered.

"Not by Morrow or Frawley or anyone else connected with them. I discounted that. If they had planned murder, there would have been no photograph taken that day, no need for their involvement whatsoever.

"Look at the last week of her life. The more I heard of it, the more it sounded a tissue of lies. True, there were explanations that fitted the things that were told me, but look how abruptly she had apparently changed her whole way of life, and place it alongside the fact that she died by violence. If the stories I was told of talks with her, of her actions, were true—and I considered they were—the two facts made an uneasy combination.

"Here is a girl who is a docile, home loving, dutiful daughter, content with keeping house for a man who has given her a good home, and to whom she is deeply grateful. Suddenly she no longer wishes to remain in that home and she also flies in the face of his anger and detestation towards conscientious objectors, by appearing in public in support of them.

"More, she is throwing out hints of a mystery man who has changed her life.

"Even if she had become involved with a conscientious objector I feel certain that a girl of the type she was, with her home background, would have been honest with her father. He would have wanted to visit her, remember. What was the sense in her leaving home to try and hide her involvement? He was bound to discover it—especially if it came to the point where she thought of marriage.

"Neither did the idea of a married man hold conviction for an instant. She had been brought up with the story of her mother's disgrace. As Mr. Calder himself claimed, the girl had been given a clear vision of what was right and what was wrong—and again, it was no use her merely running from home. Calder was bound to find out.

"It came down to two things, because I believed that the stories I had been told were true, so far as the people telling them knew—either she was romancing, or she was lying about her reason for leaving home.

"Take the first. I discounted it. Why, if there was no real reason for her leaving home would she contemplate leaving a man to whom she felt great gratitude, to loneliness, to housekeeping for himself?

"I was left with the idea of a lie. I probed back through those days preceding her wish to leave her father and home and I realised one thing. At no time had she said she loved this mystery man, or that he loved her. She had merely said that they had met and their lives had been so drastically changed that she was contemplating leaving home.

"It made no sense, for the moment, till you look closely at that conversation she had with *you*." His gaze went to the shadowed face of Chris Stowe. "Look at it closely and realise that what she had said was, 'Out there in the city one day, I met a stranger. You don't know him. I don't want you to meet him—*because he is bad, wicked.*' Think of the conversation in that context, and you follow on with, 'I met him doing something wrong and because of my knowledge he and I can never live the same sort of lives again.'

"That is a very different story altogether, when you look at the statement from the point of view of there being no love and affection in her for this mystery man.

"Go on however, to the rest of what she said, and you come up against the quite absurd statement, 'Because of all this, I have to leave home.' Immediately you are faced with your whole idea ridiculed, unless you face the fact that the man concerned lived in her home, that she was being forced to meet him every day of her life and that the position was intolerable to them both.

"It is the only solution that fitted the facts. Put Alexander Calder in the place of that mystery man and you have

Robyn Calder telling her friend, 'I have to leave home because the lives of my father and myself have been pushed right out of focus. Suddenly, out there in the city, during a demonstration, I met him and discovered in him a stranger I had never known before. Oh no,' she adds to you, Miss Stowe, 'you've never met this strange side of Alexander Calder and I don't want you to.'

"Look at that statement closely and go back through those last days of her life. Where had she changed? At what point? The answer is in the previous demonstration. In that she was so terrified of the violence that erupted that she fled the scene. She tried to find shelter in nearby buildings and was turned away. Picture her running from building to building, possibly beside herself with panic. Picture her seeing suddenly a familiar figure—a man who will surely protect her, a man whose authority would get them entrance to any building. Picture her running after him, and catching up with him and finding him—doing what?

"Calder came to this office, a frightened man. He rambled about the press having come to see him about that photo. I think it very likely they had heard, not only about the photo, but the whisper of murder that you yourselves had dragged out. If so, they would have touched on that when they interviewed him. Certainly he was a frightened man that morning in my office. He drew my attention to the student arming and he urged me to concentrate on that and offered me the job of doing exactly that.

"We can discount that he had anything to do with the arming, and the blackmailing. He wasn't afraid, anyway, of me probing into the arming. It was the talk of murder, I was sure, that had scared him into coming to me.

"Remember the girl saw him as a stranger, and an unpleasant stranger, too. That means she certainly caught him doing something wrong, criminal. What was going on? Crime, certainly, but we have dismissed the idea of blackmailing and arming the students. There were office thefts, but nobody could imagine Calder taking the incredible risk of entering offices, when he would not know how many people might be in inside rooms. The idea was nonsense.

"There was car stealing and cars and parking police are a duo, one might say, but again—no one could reasonably imagine Calder breaking the locks on parked cars and driving them away. He had his job to do. He had to wear a uniform while doing it and parking police do not drive away illegally parked cars. He is simply the Brown Bomber who drops that unpleasant bomb of a traffic fine on the unfortunate who has illegally parked. For someone to notice a respectably dressed man trying to open a car door is one thing. Even if the person has suspicions it is easier to pass by with the comfortable reflection that it is the car's owner having trouble with the lock. However, a parking policeman is noticeable. If he was seen trying to open a car the passer-by might well stop to see what was going to happen.

"So what was left? I didn't know. This morning I took to the streets of the city. It was a bright day of sunshine, if you remember, and the usual crowds were made worse by shoppers, sightseers, others brought out by the fine weather, and wherever I looked was the frustration of signs —Half Hour Parking, No Parking, No Standing, Parking Lot Full—and everywhere too the kerbsides were lined with parked cars, while circling cars moved slowly along, the drivers alert to find an empty spot.

"I was watching a parking policeman at work. I saw him writing a ticket and the woman driver, flustered, close to tears, explaining, arguing, even trying the charm of a winning, hopeful smile and soft words. It all glanced off his back. He gave her the ticket, a salute, and went on his way without a backward glance.

"Watching, I was hearing voices—Oliver Harrap speaking laughingly, mockingly, of there always being a bank clerk who would take a bribe. I was hearing Inspector Virtue's soft voice speaking of bribery, too. I could see Athol Lesie's angry face and hear him making a thrust about the police and a golden handshake, in connection with the way some clubs had apparent immunity from police harassing.

"I was remembering many things—the periodic outbursts from business firms claiming they were being forced to pay hundreds of dollars each month in traffic fines to keep their vans and their lorries to their delivery schedule; and the cries from harassed businessmen who needed their cars in the city, or wanted to drive to and from work without the crowding, the inconvenience, the frustrations of public transport.

"There was a crime Calder *might* have committed, if I could prove it. Bribery isn't unknown to either police or parking police, even if ninety-nine per cent of those forces would treat it with contempt, even if the result of being found out in accepting a bribe is very unpleasant indeed.

"I went to the area where that demonstration happened when Robyn Calder ran in panic from violence. There is a tiny strip of park there. Almost opposite, was a building housing one big firm. I went all around it and I questioned the caretaker and I discovered that like many older buildings, it had no parking lot of its own. All the kerbside outside was flanked with cars and Half Hour Parking signs.

"I went back to that little park and I sat and I waited for three hours. In all that time not one of those cars moved, not one anxious owner rushed out to discover if he had been booked for illegal parking, not one car was booked for over-stopping the time limit, and though the uniformed figure of a parking policeman paced by he totally ignored the whole line of cars.

"I thought then it was time to go to the police and I learned, as I suspected, that that area was where Alexander Calder worked.

"Go back now to that picture we were making of a terrified girl trying to find shelter. Picture her seeing her father, and following him into that building, trying to catch up with him. Doors wouldn't have stopped her in her terror and panic. She would have flung them open to reach him. What did she see and hear? Certainly Calder, and perhaps another man, in the act of passing and receiving money, and it would have been a large sum if the payment was a monthly one.

"They, or Calder alone, would have had to tell her the truth, to keep her quiet. I frankly think that it was Calder alone. If another man had been present, had heard her question and catch up with Calder, he would have been wondering since her death—and yet—it was death by demonstration, wasn't it? That is a far different thing from murder.

"If a second man, the briber, did know, I imagine he would have found some malicious amusement in the fact that Calder had been caught out by his own daugher. I doubt if he would have worried. He would have left it to Calder to keep her quiet, on the grounds of 'Like father, like daughter'.

"And after all, bribery is not a great crime. The receiving of bribes is. For a parking policeman, a bad one.

"Calder was supposed to be a loving father, yet the little I heard of him made me doubt it. One of her friends said he dominated and bossed her; another spoke of the way he humiliated her by discussing her mother's wrongdoing in public; others spoke of her spending her evenings keeping him company with a chessboard or middle-aged neighbours and cards. It wasn't the behaviour, to me, of a man who loved the girl, but rather one who was keeping her tied to him, as a housekeeper, by reminders of all she owed him. Hadn't he given her a home, when he could have turned his back on her, as her worthless mother had done?

"I think it is fairly certain that all these years she had resented those mentions of her mother; his forcing her into a quiet backstream of life that was all wrong for her age, but ... she owed him a lot for the home and the shelter and protection he had given her. So she stayed, out of duty.

"Then suddenly she sees him—the man who has taunted her with her mother's faults, who has prated of honesty, and put on a front of rectitude and honesty, as a stranger —as a man who was doing something dishonest and petty and repulsive.

"She must have rounded on him. I doubt if she would have betrayed him, but I am sure she got back at him for all those remarks about her mother, all the dullness of her life, by hinting that she could send him to prison, making his life a misery and a fear.

"He had a lot to lose, and he must have been afraid of her turning on him completely, and afraid of her letting it out unwittingly, too, and yet ... murder?

"I doubt if he would have taken the risk, have faced up to a police investigation, to probing into his life and into hers—especially if some other man knew she had found out about the bribing—but she was to attend another demonstration, in defiance of his own wishes, remember.

"So there was temptation—the chance to be rid of her, the chance of silencing her, the chance of going on peaceably, without worrying, for himself. Certainly he wouldn't have worn his uniform that day. He must have made himself look completely different, and he joined the demonstration, and he killed her."

He said grimly to the shadowed faces, "No, it isn't supposition. Calder was brought into the police station to explain why those cars had had immunity and their owners—all of them executives in the building, and all of them suddenly caught out and panic-stricken, were brought in for questioning, too.

"Just as some people are always open to bribery, so are some eager to thrust blame from themselves, if they can. Two men talked. Only too readily. Oh, they didn't know Calder was accepting a golden handshake—only that the word had gone out 'from up top' as they phrased it that the kerbside outside the building was the executives' private parking lot, for the payment of a few dollars a week each. How can Calder explain that away?

"He tried and he failed and finally he said, 'I killed her. There was a chance to do it easily and I took it.'

"I've done what you asked," he tossed at them, "and it's for you to consider whether the benefits you have won by these demonstrations were worth all the abuses and evil they've brought in their train. I don't intend to argue with you, or listen to you, or talk to you. I've done what you asked. Now leave me."

They stood hesitant. They had risen silently and then they milled, drew close together, and parted, and gazed at one another with wide, stricken eyes, and came together to stare towards his face. Only when he said again, in rising impatience, "Leave me," did they move, in a huddle, bodies close together, towards the door.

There, with the others passed through, Christine Stowe hesitated and went to speak, but she saw his hand reach out to the tape-recorder, and heard him speak. The words didn't touch on her, or anything he had said to them. Deliberately his voice droned on, speaking of other problems, as though by the sound he would drown out the memory of this last solved puzzle.

After a minute, she pulled the door to, leaving him sitting in the small pool of light, a thin, grey figure in a room of grey shadows.